FRAGMENTS OF US

First Edition November 2022

SECOND EDITION: August 2024
Published by Indies United Publishing House, LLC

Edited by Jennie Rosenblum and Jayne Southern

Compiled by Jake Cavanah
Contributing Authors: Timothy Baldwin, Laura DiNovis Berry, Jake Cavanah, Jim Infanino, Ron Kinscherf, Lisa Orban, Kasey Rogers, Guy Thair
Foreword by Richard Jacobs

ISBN 978-1-64456-753-1 [Paperback]
ISBN 978-1-64456-754-8 [ePub]

Library of Congress Control Number: 2024942561

INDIES UNITED PUBLISHING HOUSE, LLC
P.O. BOX 3071
QUINCY, IL 62305-3071
indiesunited.net

Table of Contents

For Richard
A friend, mentor, advocate,
and climate champion
until the end.

You will be missed.

Indies United Publishing House
Presents

Fragments
of US

A Multi-Author Anthology
Compiled by
Jake Cavanah

INDIES UNITED PUBLISHING HOUSE, LLC

Foreword

This Trip We're On

Life, this trip we are on, is a venture. It is through our mind's eye, our built-in camera lens, we explore the wonders of our world and its inhabitants. But there is more than today's moments, preserved like snapshots by our mind's eye. There are all the tomorrows awaiting us.

Our tomorrows depend on what we do or don't do with our todays.

When we abuse the moment, exploit the offerings of our universe, we sap our tomorrows of their vitality. Thus, our challenge is, as Thoreau once said, not merely to "look" but to "see." Seeing carries us beyond the moment – beyond the *Far Horizon* – to the tomorrows eagerly awaiting us. How does *looking* become *seeing*? By actual hands-on experience. Nothing beats it. Not the web. Not TV. Not social media. Nothing, absolutely nothing, beats it.

In my writings, I call it "dirty hands, wet feet learning."

I have been fortunate. I practiced law for some 6 decades. I have trekked, photographed the seven continents. *Democracy of Dollars* and other books I have written have been shaped and motivated by these life-changing, hands-on personal experiences. Our project at Stetson University College of Law, the *Dick and Joan Jacobs Public Interest Law Clinic for Democracy and the Environment* came about in answer to the lessons learned, and our realization of our responsibilities to pass to future generations the opportunities to be guided by similar experiences. Our future as a democracy depends upon it.

Dick Jacobs

Bennett Springs, Missouri
Abe

by Ron Kinscherf

Abe rolled over and opened his eyes. The digital numbers on his alarm clock were dark. He sighed and grabbed his wristwatch off the nightstand. He wiped the sleep from his eyes, looked at the watch, and moaned.

"Bloody 7:25 AM." He swung his feet over the side of the bed and turned on the lamp on the nightstand. Nothing.

"Jesus Christ. I guess no fishing this morning." He put his feet in his slippers, went to the front door of his trailer and peered out. Not a single light.

He opened the door and headed to the back of the trailer. Jerry, from the cabin on his left, yelled, "Hey,

Abe, you want a cup of joe?"

Waving him off, Abe continued to the back of his trailer. He pulled the cable on his generator. Nothing. He pulled again. Nothing. He stood up … stretched his back a bit … and pulled again. The generator started. "Hot damn," Abe muttered and turned around.

"Here's a cup, Abe."

"Jerry, you about scared the piss out of me." Abe continued right past Jerry.

"Crazy about the power," Jerry continued. "No storm or nothing. Even the lodge doesn't have power. The fishin' siren didn't even go off this morning, but I'm sure you noticed that."

Abe hadn't thought about that. He turned, snatched the cup, mumbled, "Thanks," and went into his trailer.

Abe flipped a switch and the lights flickered on. He sat at the little dining table and sipped his coffee. He pondered on what could have happened to the power … tree limb? … couldn't be … no storm. Squirrel? "I bet it was a squirrel." He chuckled. "Damn squirrels." He'd fought many a war at home over the squirrels and the bird feeders.

Cream. He wanted cream. He stood and made his way to the refrigerator. Behind a fish-shaped magnet was the perfect family picture. The whole family caught a fish that day. The first time. The girls in pigtails and overalls. Abe and his wife, Martha. All holding that day's catch. He flipped the picture over: April of 1994. Everyone happy. Everyone getting along. If it could only last forever. Abe put the picture back.

"OK, where were we." Cream. He opened the door. "Shit." He remembered the power. "Wonder how long it's been off?"

Abe threw on a shirt, tugged a pair of jeans over his pajama pants, and grabbed his fishing hat and keys. "Might as well head into town and see what the hell is going on."

The drive to Lebanon, Missouri, would take around twenty minutes or so.

Abe had been coming to Bennett Springs, Missouri, for over 50 years straight. First, with his pops. Then with his brothers. Later, his wife. And when the girls arrived, they tagged along, too … even as babies. Fifty some years and this was his first solo trip.

Bennett Springs had some of the best trout fishing in the Midwest. Just south of the Lake of the Ozarks, fishermen from all over the country come to throw their lines into the Niangua River.

Abe turned left out of the campground onto Route 66, the Will Rogers Highway. Not much traffic today.

A cloudy sky made it darker than most mornings. To the west, it was really dark, but he didn't see clouds: just a dark, grayish haze. "Peculiar." His eyes flicked back and forth to his rear-view mirror. "What the hell is that?"

He lived in Central Illinois his whole life and figured he'd seen every type of weather event. But, for the life of him, Abe had no idea what he was looking at. "Martha, I wish you could see this."

The closer he got to Lebanon, the more the traffic picked up. A lot. Trailers, RVs, even some town folk. "And it's Thursday, not a typical getaway day."

Tapping his blinker, Abe turned into the gravel parking lot of Sarge's, a little diner off 66. He shut the

5

truck off, left the keys on the dash and climbed out. In all the years he'd been coming to this place, he had no idea why it was called Sarge's. The current Sarge wasn't in the service; the dumbass had a degree in English Literature. Martha thought that maybe his grandpa had been in the service. The little bell jingled as he opened the door.

At the bar, he picked up a menu and took a seat. There wasn't a soul in the place. "What the hell is—?"

From the kitchen he heard, "Abe! What are you doing here?"

He said, "Well, Sarge, I was hoping to get some food. Where the hell is—?"

Sarge came hustling out of the kitchen, wiping his hands with a towel. "Abe, I wasn't sure if I would see you this April. But I sure am glad to see ya. Really sorry about Martha. I wanted to get to the—"

Abe cut him off. "Thanks." He appreciated the sentiments, but dammit, didn't anyone have anything else to talk about? "Where the hell is everybody? What's going on?"

Sarge stared at Abe, "You haven't heard?"

"Heard what?" Abe answered.

"Just a second. You need coffee. I got a fresh pot that needs drinkin'."

Abe stared at Sarge as he turned, grabbed a cup, and the pot of coffee, an old glass one with a big dark stain around the bottom. "Sarge, what in the hell is going on around here."

Sarge poured a cup, set it in front of Abe along with a couple of creams, put the pot down next to him on top of a towel and said, "One more second."

"Sarge!" Abe was getting a bit peeved. Sarge selected a cup for himself, scooted around the bar and sat next to Abe.

"Oh, wait." Sarge hopped up, ran around the bar, and returned with the TV remote.

"Sarge, if you don't tell me what's going on, I'm going to slap that mustache off your face. I may be old but—"

The TV came to life. "Holy hell, what is that?"

Sarge just stared at the muted TV. Lava everywhere. Cars on highways, bumper to bumper. Reporters covered in what looked like ash. Maps of the United States. Different shades of red west of the Mississippi. Kansas City was orange, Columbia Missouri yellow, as was Bennett Springs.

"Sarge, what is going on?"

"Abe … there's this caldera … was this caldera in Yellowstone and … wait, a caldera is—"

"I know what a caldera is. It's the hole at the top of a volcano."

"Well, I had to look it up, I have degree in Lit, so I had to Google and—"

"Not important. Move along."

"Sorry. So, this volcano erupted. Wasn't supposed to. It just happened. There's no power anywhere in the West. One third of the US is covered in ash. Abe, didn't you feel it last night?"

Abe watched the TV and shook his head. Since Martha passed, he'd taken a sleeping pill with a shot of Jack to get to sleep.

"Lord, Abe, it knocked half the bottles off the bar shelf." Sarge pointed to the broken glass on the floor behind the bar. A mop leaned against the beer coolers.

Sarge continued, "So, the President has issued a nationwide disaster thing. All national guard units have been deployed. The religious freaks are yelling that the Book of Revelation warned about this. The Republicans are blaming the Democrats. The Democrats are blaming the Republicans. Oh, and the Chinese, they—"

Sarge rambled on. Abe's kids. His grandkids. He looked at his phone. No coverage. Of course. The power grid is shut down. Cell service is shut down.

"Sarge." Sarge kept on talking. "Sarge!"

He stopped and stared at Abe. "Thank you. Where are your workers?"

"People are freaked, Abe. Just freaked. They've packed up and left. The ash is coming. It should be here by midnight at the latest. No more sunshine. Breathing may be difficult."

Abe threw a dollar on the counter and stood up. "I best be on my way."

Sarge picked up the dollar and put it in Abe's breast pocket. He put a hand on each of Abe's shoulders. "Abe. Again, I am soooo sorry about Martha."

"Thanks, Sarge."

"What you gonna do? Where you gonna go?"

"Well, I'm thinking I better find the kids." One of Abe's daughters lived in Champaign, Illinois, on the eastern side of the state. And his other daughter, the youngest, lived in Terre Haute, Indiana, a few hours from Champaign.

Abe opened the door and was about to let go when he heard Sarge call out. "See you in the Fall, you old fart."

Abe smiled, nodded, and headed to his truck.

In the 20 minutes that Abe spent in Sarge's, the whole county must have found out this wasn't some little old earthquake. It took Abe twice as long to get back to the campground, which included 15 minutes just to make a left turn out of Sarge's.

Pandemonium greeted Abe at the campground. "Oh, Martha, if you could see this. Somebody must have spilled the beans."

Women hugged their children and sobbed. Men heaved their belongings into their trucks. And the reverse. Men sobbing with children and women throwing stuff in their trucks. Neighbors hugged neighbors. Gravel flew as campers fishtailed out of their parking spots.

Abe carefully pulled into his spot in front of his trailer and stepped out. He looked around at the chaos one more time and ambled into his home away from home.

He plopped into his recliner. "Well, Bessie, time to say goodbye." Abe and Martha had named the trailer some 20 years ago when they purchased the thing from the Gierstens. The Gierstens had shown up one Spring in a fancy new Keystone RV. Abe moseyed over and asked Al what he intended to do with the old one. Al honestly said he hadn't thought about it. Ten minutes later, it belonged to Abe and Martha.

Martha laughed at that story every time the couple discussed it. Bessie? They named it after the first car they purchased ... a used 1960-something Pontiac.

Everything Abe saw reminded him of Martha. The bunk beds. The small kitchen. The owl salt and pepper shakers. Abe smiled. Martha's mother thought the shakers would bring them bad luck because owls were Satanic symbols.

Abe pulled himself up, opened his duffle bag and began packing. He grabbed his little Coleman cooler and threw in some beer, water, cold cuts, and bread. The generator had been on long enough to harden some cubes so they resembled something like ice. He tossed some of that in also.

He strategically put the bottle of Jack in a wool sock and placed it in the duffle. He gave the place the once over. Turning, he said, "See ya, Bessie," and walked out of the door.

A few seconds later, he dashed back in, plucked the picture off the fridge and ran back out. His hand was the last thing to leave Bessie as it flicked off the overhead light.

• ———— ·☣· ———— •

The pickup rolled along on Highway 44, east towards Rolla, Missouri and onto St. Louis. Abe was listening to Martha's favorite, *Peter, Paul & Mary's Greatest Hits*. He chuckled as "If I Had a Hammer" played. Martha used to tease, "If I had a hammer, Abe, you'd always be doing them dishes!"

"Gas. What the hell am I going to do for gas?" With no power, the gas pumps wouldn't work. "Shit, Martha. I've got half a tank."

He flipped out the CD and turned on the radio. "KMOX in St. Louis. PLEASE. PLEASE. PLEASE."

KMOX AM Radio, the "Voice of St. Louis," blasted 50,000 watts of talk radio throughout the Midwest. The signal covered the eastern half of Missouri and southern Illinois.

Fiddling with the dial, Abe drove. "C'mon. C'mon. C'mon. Finally." Abe had a faint signal mixed with static. "Tell me the scoop."

He expected KMOX to do nothing but cover the disaster. What the heck else mattered at this point? What he made out was mostly about the national side of things. Two feet of ash covered Wyoming and the surrounding states. The Santa Ana Winds had helped California by pushing the ash inland, so coverage was not as heavy, but they were also without power.

Lava continued to spread. Fires were out of control. State of emergency. National Guard. Stay calm. Listen to law enforcement. Blah. Blah. Blah.

"On the local front—" said an obviously flustered news anchor.

Abe couldn't imagine. She had worked her whole life to get this great opportunity to work at a nationally recognized radio station and now this disaster. Did she have kids? Parents? Were they safe? Obviously, there is loyalty to the listener, but when does sanity prevail?

"—the forecast for ash distribution continues to be murky. Kansas City is starting to see accumulation. Parts of Central Missouri are seeing some ash. Ash continues to escape from the crater of the Yellowstone volcano as eruptions are ongoing, albeit smaller than the initial blast. Experts are unsure when the eruptions will stop."

"That's not good," Abe murmured.

"As you know, the entire power grid west of the Mississippi is down. KMOX's leadership had the foresight to have another power source on the east side of the river, allowing us to stay on the air and continue to serve you, our listener."

"That's good," Abe thought. "The kids should be OK."

"There is no good information on when power may be restored to any of the areas currently experiencing outages. Estimates of over 100 million are without power. The US Government and the country's utility companies are meeting 24x7 to urgently come up with a plan. We will update you as we receive more information."

"As for the weather, expect, in the short term, consistent temperatures lower than normal and very little sunshine until the ash starts to dissipate. If you encounter trouble breathing, try to locate a medical expert and stay inside. If you do need to go outside, a face covering is recommended."

Abe muttered, "Try to find a medical expert? We are in some sort of mess, Martha, aren't we?"

The information was nothing revelatory to Abe. No power means a lot of nothing. Abe turned down the volume. The traffic continued to pick up. His speed was steady, but he worried about when he hit Rolla and how much worse it would get with 20,000 plus citizens hitting the road east.

Maybe get off the main roads? Abe checked his phone. Google would help. But of course … no signal.

Abe's mind wandered as he rolled through Central Missouri. The kids had to be worried. Payphone maybe? Abe chuckled. "Payphones are gone like the dodo."

The kids had taken turns to check on him since Martha's passing. Abe wished they would stop, but he didn't have the heart to tell them. With every nightly call, reminders of the agony came tumbling back. They hurt, too, and they felt guilty for not being with him. But it's been four months. They need to get on with their lives. Abe did, too.

Cars had pulled over on the shoulder. Some occupied, some not. More and more people walked along the road carrying their belongings. Should he pick someone up and help? End-of-the-world movies, where people start to turn on each other, flashed through his mind.

A quarter tank. "I wonder what the optimum speed is to save the most gas?"

He saw an open gas station. He took the ramp. "Well, will you look at that line, Martha." At least 40 cars queued up in front of him. "Don't think I have a choice."

The dual pump station in Doolittle, Missouri, named after the famous aviator during World War II who bombed Japan in the Pacific Theatre, sat about 15 minutes west of Rolla.

A man approached Abe as he sat in line. He rolled down his window.

"Good afternoon, sir. You lookin' for some gas?"

"Yep. Not much else out here." The man had on a typical gas station shirt with his name, Sam, stitched on it.

"I hope you don't mind waiting."

"Don't have much of a choice."

"Well, gas will cost you $20.00 a gallon. And we are only taking cash."

Abe responded, "What the hell? That's just—"

Sam raised his hands in defense. "Sir, supply and demand. I have no idea when I will get another shipment, if I get another shipment. I need to get what I can when I can. Once my tanks are empty, I will be joining you and everyone else and heading out of Dodge."

Hard to argue with that. Abe took a deep breath and exhaled. Fortunately for Abe, he didn't believe in credit cards and always carried cash. "So, how are the pumps even working?"

"I have a fishing camp over by Poole Hollow. Have a generator and grabbed it at dawn. Fueled it up and here we are. Lucky I still have the old pumps that aren't on that crazy computer shit. My wife is up there and will take care of you." Sam stuck his hand in the window. Abe shook it. "Sir, God speed on your travels."

"Good luck to you, Sam," Abe replied.

Abe grabbed his cooler, popped a beer, made himself a sandwich and waited.

• ———— ·☣· ———— •

Ping!   Ping!   Ping!   Ping! Ping! Ping! Ping! Ping! Ping! Ping! Ping!

"Holy Mother of God!" Abe about jumped through the windshield. Thank the Lord for seatbelts. Messages on his cell phone. First a couple. Then like a Gatling gun non-stop for five minutes.

Abe had avoided St. Louis after hearing about the

traffic congestion as travelers crossed the Mississippi to what they hoped was salvation. So, he'd skirted northeast and chosen the old routes he used to take with his dad before Eisenhower built the highway system. He was between Bowling Green and Louisiana when his phone came to life.

He glanced at the device and smiled. Texts. Voicemails. Family. He pulled over on the shoulder. He hit *1. Speed dial for his eldest Mary.

"Dad! … Oh my God! … Dad, where are you? … Jackie, it's Dad! … Dad, you OK? ... Jackie, dammit, it's Dad! … Dad, are you OK? … Jackie! Dad. Let me put you on speaker phone! Oh, my God. Oh, my God. Jackie!"

"Shit Mary … I am right here. Dad? You, OK? Where are you?"

"Language, Jacqueline."

"Dad … there's been a fucking explosion! A real mother fucker of an explosion. If I want to curse, I will goddamn curse. Now, where the hell are you?"

Despite the situation, Abe couldn't help but laugh.

"Dammit, Dad. This isn't funny."

"I know, sweetie … I know. I'm somewhere in eastern Missouri between Bowling Green and Louisiana."

"So, where's that?" Mary asked.

"Girls, remember where we used to get those chocolate dip cones with Papi? Right around there."

Silence. Just some breathing. Then tears. "Girls? Are you there?"

"Dad. Why didn't you call? We didn't know where you were. We didn't know—"

Silence.

"Girls, without power there's no cell service. No cell service ... no—"

"Oh, yeah. Hadn't thought about that," mumbled Mary.

Abe sat silent for a moment. "Girls. There was really nothing to worry about. I've been to Bennett."

Jackie scolded her dad. "Dad. We told you, you shouldn't have gone on the trip. You're old. And alone. You could have broken a—"

"Jackie—" Mary tried to jump in.

"Mary! You agreed. Dad wasn't and IS NOT ready to travel alone ... particularly to the middle of nowhere."

Mary tried again. "Jackie, now is not the time to—"

"Dad's too frail. What if he tripped in the trailer? Or fell in the river? Snakes. There are snakes everywhere."

Abe sat quietly while his daughters argued about his ability to walk and talk. After a few moments, there was a pause. "So, where are you two at?"

"We are at my place ... in Champaign. Jackie brought the kids as soon as the explosion happened."

They're together. Good. The girls got along. Barely. And it didn't get any better after Martha passed. They talked or argued about what should happen with the house. Should Abe move? If he did, where to? And it was worse while Martha was sick. This doctor. This hospital. This treatment plan. None of it mattered anyway. By the time the cancer was discovered, it was too late. She just had a few months. Then the funeral. Oh, the funeral. Sometimes illness brings family together. Martha's cancer did not. But they are together now. Maybe it takes the largest natural disaster in millennia, but they are together.

Jackie said, barely audible, "Dad, are you OK? Really, OK?"

"Yes, dear. I'm perfectly fine. I even went potty by myself."

Jackie chuckled and said, "Dammit, Dad." And then she was crying again. Abe teared up too.

After a moment or two, Mary asked softly, "Dad, what's the plan?"

"Well, I was thinking about joining you two. If there's room."

"Yes, Dad. We will make room." Abe could see the snark on Mary's face.

"OK, as long as I can get gas, I should be in Champaign in four hours. Depending on traffic. After then we'll play it by ear. Come up with a game plan."

"OK." Mary mumbled. After a few seconds, she quietly said, "I miss—WE miss Mom—really bad."

"We all do, sweetie. We all do."

Emails from The Dark

by Jim Infantino

Felicia Thompson, Oberlin, OH

Subject: Thanksgiving break

Hi, Mom,

First year here is going great.
I love my Music Theory professor. I'm
learning modal scales on the cello.
The level of talent of my classmates
is intimidating, but I persevere. My
Ancient History and Philosophy 101
classes are cool. They work well
together. I'm thinking of taking a
Creative Writing class next semester.
I know Dad wanted me to take some
Engineering classes, but I don't
think it's for me. Oberlin is so good
at the arts and liberal arts, and I
want to steep in that stuff first and
see where it leads me.

The weather on campus has been
gorgeous. I picked up a single-speed
bike on Buy Nothing/Sell Nothing and
am whisking about the campus and
taking short trips into town. The
campus is pretty flat, which is great
because I'm way out of shape. The
fall foliage is in full swing, and
it's GORGEOUS, but I have to watch
out for the wet leaves after it
rains. And no, I don't have a helmet
yet, but I'm looking to pick one up
soon. They're like $60 at the local
bike shop. Can I put it on the card?

The only problem is that I HATE
my roommate. She's staring at me as I
write this and picking her nose. Ick.
She wears these handmade dresses with

stars and stuff on them with tassels that drape down to her ankles and are all way too big. She never brushes her hair. It's a tangled mess and I think she's starting to get dreads, which is fine if that's what she's going for, but it looks like a rat's nest under all that frizz. I don't know why I got stuck in this room with her. There are plenty of other women here who dress as badly as she does. She should be with one of them. She burns this disgusting incense during the day and snores at night. I'm in hell.

So, can you book a flight home to Rapid City for me? I want to leave the Tuesday before Thanksgiving and come home to be with you, Dad, Sunny, and Brian for the break. I'm dreaming of your sweet potato casserole. I can't wait to see you all.

Love, Felicia

Re: Thanksgiving break

Dearest Felicia,
Of course we can book you a flight back. I'm checking on it now.

Do you want a stopover in Chicago or Denver? Denver is a bit cheaper. Can you find a ride to the airport in Cleveland, or is Akron better? I think the one from Akron stops over in Charlotte, which might make the trip too long.

PLEASE buy that helmet. Put it on the card. The last thing you need is a concussion or worse. Please wear it when you ride. It's serious. You need to protect your brain, sweetheart. Remember what happened to Joey Tartaglia when he hit that tree on his motorcycle? His mom has to spoon-feed him and he can't remember what day it is. Don't make me do that for you.

So sorry to hear about your roommate woes. All I can tell you is that it's part of the freshman (ugh, that word) experience. Your father and I both had roommates we disliked when we entered college. Next year, you'll be able to pick someone you like. For now, be glad you were placed into a double and make the most of it. Practice tolerance and patience. I know it's hard.

Those courses sound fine to me. Your dad wants you to study physics and science because those topics are near and dear to him. I'm sure he's happy that you're not studying mining. He's become a bit of a pariah at the college here for telling his students that they are in a dead-end field. I'm not sure I agree with him. I hope it doesn't get him fired.

The big news here is we've traded in our Suburban for an electric truck! Can you believe it? We had to go to Fargo for the one we wanted. It's nice, but I worry about the range. It took two charges to get it home, one in Bismarck and one in the middle of nowhere. Who'd have thought there were any charging stations in the Dakotas? The great thing is that we don't have to worry about gas prices anymore. We plug it in at home overnight and it's pennies on the dollar to "fill the tank." So cool. It's silver. Can't wait to pick you up from the airport in it. Oh, another problem is it seats four. I guess you, Sunny, and Brian will need to crowd into the back seat when we go out to Tally's.

My business has been slow. Rapid City is a hot real estate market right now, but there's no inventory. Since we moved from Madison, I've been longing for more variety in the places I show. I have one house on the market and it's a snoozer. It's hard to get worked up about it. It'll probably go for above asking when we have the open house this weekend, so that's something.

Don't be a stranger! Remember, you can text us anytime, day or night. I know you're not a texter, but I keep checking my app for a message from you, so maybe send me a sticker or a photo or anything at all. We miss you terribly and are so proud of you.

Are you eating well?

Can we do a video call sometime soon? Tomorrow night, maybe?

Love, Mom.

Re: Re: Thanksgiving break

Hey, Mom,

Sorry about the lack of texts. I've actually been really busy here. The work is hard and the reading is insane. My friends bug me all the time on my app and I never respond. I don't like typing on my phone. I know I'm weird. I just sent you a picture of the quad. So nice today. I got to lie on a blanket and read between

Econ and Phil.

Stevenson has everything I want. I'm eating well, but there are like, all these fried options :-) and it's hard to ignore them sometimes. I don't want to gain weight like they say we all will. That's part of the reason I was happy to get my bike. Speaking of which, I need to oil the chain, right? It squeaks. Can you ask Dad what kind of oil I need? Is it grease or oil? I know nothing about taking care of it. Dad always looked after our bikes back in Wisconsin. It's a Specialized, if that matters.

I can't believe you got an electric truck! That's beyond. I can't wait to drive it. Did you let Sunny drive it yet? I bet Brian can't wait to get his permit.

Hey, I saw something in the Rapid City Journal about earthquakes? How is that even a thing there? Are you all okay?

Love,
Felicia

Re: Re: Re: Thanksgiving break

Darling Felicia,

Yes, we've been getting tremors. They happen here, apparently. The windows in the house I'm showing this weekend are cracked. Terrible timing. I've never experienced earthquakes before. I didn't know what was happening. I thought it was a train passing nearby at first, but then I realized we don't live anywhere near the tracks and it just kept coming. Your dad rushed us all under a doorway until it stopped. We had some broken plates and pictures. I thought the house was going to come down. It was pretty frightening. The first one was a magnitude five and there were aftershocks. I can't imagine how bad a bigger one would be. A five was about all I could handle. The aftershocks mess with your head. Brian thought it was 'fun.' Sunny is a little traumatized. All things considered, we're fine, but we will have to reframe some pictures and replace the dishware. The photo of your nana and bapa was ripped down the middle. I think I can get it repaired in town.

Your dad has been distracted since the quake. He's concerned that we weren't the only ones to feel it. There was a bad one in Salt Lake you might have heard about around the same time and one in Boise. He's been emailing all night with a geologist he knows in California. He won't tell me why. I wouldn't worry, though. He's always into one disastrous scenario or another. I want to get the home I'm showing repaired and back on the market. Oh, and I got you a flight from Cleveland, stopping in Denver. I emailed you the tickets.

Your dad says you need to go to the bike shop and get some bike chain oil. He said not to use 3-in-One or any other hardware store oil. The wrong type of lubricant gunks up the works. I hope that helps.

More news from the Thompson home: we're thinking of adding solar panels to the roof! Your dad says we can drive for free if we get them installed. Aren't we quite the eco-friendly family now? Not sure what the neighbors will think.

Anyway, aside from the scare, everything here is fine, fine, fine, as Mike Doughty says. You probably don't know that reference. I should send you some Mp3s. Old people music. You know what an Mp3 is right? ;-)

Stay away from the fried foods!

All our love,

FRAGMENTS OF US

Mom.

Subject: omg, are you okay?

Mom,
I heard there were more
earthquakes. My roomie is freaking
out about it. She says Wyoming is
going to explode. She's an idiot, but
I'm worried. Let me know you're
alright.

Felicia

Re: omg, are you okay?

Hi, my sweet,
Well, we had another series of
them. The first shock was a 6.2,
which is much, much worse than a 5.0.
I think we have some structural
damage to our house and the place I
was showing is a complete wreck. Your
dad got a cut on his forehead from a
piece of falling plaster. He's okay,
but we're all shook up here. We'll be
okay, but it was a bad one.
Frankly, I think you should tell

27

your roommate to hush up. That kind of disaster talk does nothing but frighten the people around you. She should know better.

This time, Brian didn't think the earthquake was fun. The high school is closed because one of the floors collapsed, and it's no longer safe for students. Your brother is sitting in his closet playing games on his phone. I can't get him to come out of there. Sunny thinks we should move. She's like your dad in that way, always imagining the worst. They will both calm down before long, but you might want to call them. They'd love to hear from you.

On that note, it looks like there's a possibility we might be driving across the country to see you soon, so you might not need to fly here after all. Your dad thinks we should take a road trip. It seems a little sudden to me, but it would be fun to see you on the campus. I hope we can find enough charging stations to get us all the way to Ohio. I looked into canceling the tickets, but it costs as much to reschedule them as buying a new flight. Airlines —they're the worst.

We adore you,

Mom.

Re: Re: omg, are you okay?

I will call you all tonight, I promise. I'm sitting in my Phil 101 class right now, waiting for Professor Kosman to show up. He's usually here before the class starts, but he's late today. I can't believe a floor of the school collapsed! That's crazy.

I'm glad you are all coming here to visit. Do you think you'll be here for the Thanksgiving break? If so, it'll be neat showing you the campus when it's empty, but it would be more fun to be able to show you around when some of my friends and professors are here. I'm a little confused as to why you're coming so suddenly.

If you do come, I want to try driving the new truck while you're here. Anyway, gotta go, Kosman finally showed up.
Love,
Felicia

Text message from: Dad

Don't respond. Get to the store
NOW. Buy as many cans of food and
bottles of water as you can carry.
Stay inside. We're coming to get you.

Subject: What is going on?

Hi, Dad,
I tried texting you back, but
none of them are going through. Do
you have your phone turned off?
I remember our prep exercises in
case of a blizzard, so when I saw
your text, I did exactly what you
said, or I tried to.
I biked to the supermarket with
my backpack and the place was mobbed.
I got some dried fruit and four cans
of cream of mushroom soup, but almost
all of the other cans of food were
gone. I added two cans of green beans
to my pack, that's all. I managed to
get three liters of bottled water,

sparkling, and I was in line to check out when people started grabbing things off the shelf and running back to their cars. When I was three away from the front of the line, the cashier pocketed all the cash in the drawer and walked out the front door. Everyone was all "what the?" So then it got totes crazy and I took what I could carry and got out of there. I got lots of pasta and oats, some frozen dinners and Twizzlers.

Now I have no idea what's happening. I heard some weird theories standing in line, but I don't believe any of them. Some people said it was a major hurricane coming our way, others said it was nuclear war. One tall skinny guy I recognized from my Econ class said we were headed into another ice age. I asked him what his phone said, because I left mine on the bed after I saw your text, and he said, "Ice age. Say goodbye to global warming."

When I got back to my dorm, I found a note from my roomie saying, "Good luck, and farewell." Lots of her things are still here, but I noticed her backpack and mandolin are missing. Her piglet-shaped pillow is gone, too, so she's probably out of my hair for a while. Maybe she has a

31

boyfriend. Ewww.

Okay, I checked the news on my phone and there's a hundred crazy stories about a mega-colossal eruption in Yellowstone? Holyfukinshit! All the news vids say not to panic, but I'm feeling like a good panic might very well be in order at the moment. I wish I had gotten more water. Heck, I wish I had grabbed some gin! (Sorry, Mom.)

They say western Wyoming is now a small inland sea of molten rock? The caldera is 45 miles wide and spewing lava into the air? How can this be real? How far is the eruption from home? Are you all okay? Where are you?

Send me a text or email when you get this. I'm pretty freaked out.

F.

Re: What is going on?

Well, I will hand it to my missing roommate. Her name is Sandy by the by. I don't think I mentioned that before.

Anyhoo, she left a bottle of rye whiskey on her bookshelf, hidden behind her copy of 'The Naked Man' by Claude Lévi-Strauss, and I am ever so grateful for that. I'm sorry, Mom, but yes, I am drunk and I am drunk because I am PETRIFIED THAT I HAVEN'T HEARD FROM YOU YET AND WYOMING IS ON FIRE AND IT'S RIGHT NEXT TO WHERE WE LIVE AND

Just text or call or respond to this, PLEASE.

Please.

I love you.

Subject: New protocols

Mom, Dad, Sunny, and Brian,

It's been three days and I haven't heard from any of you. I wrote a few dozen emails that were mostly gibberish, but I deleted them all last night because they clearly never made it to you and they contained little more than my repetitive pleas for assurance you were all okay. The final ones were ugly and angry and I would be grateful if you never mention them to me if you ever see them. On top of the emails, I texted you all a few hundred times, but each text came back with that awful exclamation point in a circle icon that has started to remind me of a butt crack.

I am aware that there are some conclusions I could draw from my inability to reach any of you, but I've decided to put them to one side. For now, you are my Schrödinger family. I have suspended you in a state of both and neither being and or non-being.

Whether or not you ever get these, I'm going to write you about what is happening here, because it's a lot.

I imagine you guessed that, by now, all classes have been canceled for the year, but we've been told we're welcome to stay in our dorms if we have nowhere to go. That applies to anyone whose home is buried under four feet of volcanic ash or can't manage their way past an erupting supervolcano.

The college is empty. Those who live on the East Coast have driven or found rides back home. Some of the West Coast students are driving around south or up through Canada. The international students left first to get to a big enough airport before

the ash makes that sort of travel
impossible. It's only us Mountain
Time people here now.

Sandy made it to Vermont with
her family. She texted me, wishing me
luck. I told her to fuck off and I
regret doing that. I was jealous.

We have a small crew at the
cafeteria and a minimal staff from
administration. That's a godsend. For
now, it feels like staying on campus
for fall break, which I know it's
not.

Be alive,
F.

Re: New Protocols

The sky to the west is seriously
dark. I noticed the haze on the
horizon previously, but I guess I was
only looking at the leading edge of
the dust cloud. I got on top of our
building this morning and the sunrise
to the east was burnt orange. That's
not right. That means the dust from
Yellowstone has already enveloped us
in four days. It's spreading out

everywhere, dissipating from the eruption, but there is plenty more coming. I will climb back up to the roof tonight to see what the sunset looks like.

Felicia

Re: Re: New Protocols

You know that part in the movie where somebody sees something the others don't, and yells "Guys?" Well, that was me tonight. I started watching the sun's path around four this afternoon, and it changed from yellow to burnt orange before it hit the dust cloud, high in the sky. It was brown just before it vanished, setting behind a horrifying mass of unbelievable billowing blackness. You think that because you're a couple of thousand miles away from something, you can regard it passively and from a safe distance. Not this thing. This thing will be on us soon. Dad, I'm guessing this is the ash? Are you all inside it? I'm petrified, for you, for me, for everyone.

I love you,
F.

Subject: Invasion

This morning, the whole town moved onto campus. It feels that way, at least. They showed up with full cars and occupied the dorms. I woke up to a knock on my double and found a family of five waiting outside in the hallway. They were polite and moved on. I locked my door and kept it locked. I walked down to the dining center to find it filled with families. Some of the parents had guns. That can't be good. They were arguing with the staff who keep us fed. I overheard talk of securing the supplies against outsiders who might come and take the food by force. Funny, that's what I thought was already happening.

More later, someone's knocking on the door again.

F.

A FUTURE HISTORY

Re: Invasion

I'm back. I met some people from town and I think that it's actually a good thing that they came to campus. We're kinda sitting ducks.

The ash cloud on the horizon is grayer and taller. Franklin, the townie who knocked on my door before, was up on the roof with me this afternoon, and he said that the color and height probably meant we were already well under it, and it would start raining ash tomorrow. I'm guessing you are all inside that thing. I try not to think about it. If it does rain ash here, then it's already dumping out west. That means the sky's dark all day long out in the Dakotas, Minnesota, and Iowa, probably. Ash all along the roads, I'm guessing. I know Dad knows all about this, which is why I have hope. I think about our new electric truck and whether that's a problem now. All those solar panels everywhere, with a lot less sun to collect.

Franklin says the ash will dim the sun for a year or more. Things'll get nasty, he said, and that's why some of the locals have come here to secure the cafeteria. They think the college is more defensible than the town. I hope he's right.

We get some news from the east on the web. It's hard to make out what's real from what's conspiracy. There's a surprising amount of biblical apocalypse stuff on the regular news. Maybe there's nobody in charge, or different people came in. My favorite newscasters have gone underground, sending out newsletters, and tweeting. The global network is working, with all the social media companies, but even though the universities are hubs for the internet, we don't always have a live connection. The center of the world seems to have moved to London and Berlin, where this is all still far, far away. Franklin says it won't stay that way for long.

The upshot is that there's a hole in the middle of the United States and it's throwing stuff into the air at an alarming pace, most of it moving east with the weather, but a lot falling west and north, as the heat is causing anomalies in the jet stream. So, it's still moving this way, but slower, and it's messing up

A FUTURE HISTORY

California, Oregon, Washington, British Columbia, and even Alaska. Lots of Idaho and Wyoming, and parts of Colorado and Utah are completely gone. The climatologists are all over the news now, talking about a mini ice age. They say it happened before in the twelfth century or something. Others say this will be way worse than that.

The doomsday preppers are super excited, tho. That gets mixed in with the biblical evangelical wrath of God stuff. Lots of them are yelling, "I told ya so," to anyone who will rebroadcast it. I think this is good news. If they have their basements stocked with cans, they're less likely to come and try to take ours. Franklin agrees. I think the people we have to worry about are the ones who didn't have a plan, only a whole lot of guns and ammo.

Anyway, I'm rambling here. I want to put down what I understand about what's going on. All I want is to see you all again. I keep looking for your truck pulling up on campus. I told Franklin not to shoot you.

Please be alright. I love you so much,

                    Felicia

Subject: **Heat**

It's been quite a week.

I've been busy here, shoring things up, lending a hand and protecting our growing community. The internet is growing increasingly spotty. I may not be able to send this, but writing to you keeps me sane.

Electricity has also become unreliable. The college depends on the city grid for lights and such, and we've had blackouts lately. I charge my laptop when I can, but I don't know how long the current will flow. I think the power is going on and off all over the eastern half of the US. The campus has solar panels but they're generating less power every day because of the dust cloud. People are referring to it as 'The Dark,' even though it's hard to see the change in the daytime sky, but the effect is real. The Dark is cooling things down a lot. It's been below freezing the past few days, and that usually doesn't happen until after December. Thank goodness the campus finished its geothermal heating upgrade before this happened, or we'd all be in worse trouble than we are.

The biggest problem is refrigeration. I've been working with the people living here to move our food from the fridge to a cold storage unit we've created in the back of a classroom building. The first thing we had to do was remove all the heat from that half of the building, which wasn't a problem, but we also had to block all of the vents and make sure to keep the light out to avoid ambient heat. Essentially, we made a large dark cave. Then we packed all the ice we could generate in sawdust and moved the food in from the cafeteria freezers and refrigerators before the power completely fails. This should keep our stores cold until summer, which is longer than the stuff will last, given all the new mouths to feed. We still have gas for cooking and there are some backup generators that run on diesel. We need to find more fuel.

I know all this not because I've become an overnight engineering genius but because we have nightly meetings to keep up to date with what is happening. We have become a little

or not so little town. There are
about sixteen hundred of us so far.
We let some people in and turn others
away depending on whether we think
they will help or hurt our chances of
survival. Some people don't play well
with others. We try to pick those who
do.

Our town has a governing council
of twelve members who switch out at
regular intervals so that nobody gets
comfortable enough with their power
to start abusing it. Some of the
people who came from the town are the
professors who lived nearby. None of
them are mine. Others live in town
but work here, and some view the
prospect of survival more likely in a
closer-knit community than in their
culs-de-sac and private homes.

I've heard we've already
repelled an attack. Our numbers here
were a plus against the half-dozen
trucks full of wackos. We had one
casualty before we blew out their
tires and took their weapons. I've
been told the woman who was shot will
live, but her recovery will take a
while. We were lucky. Don't worry; it
happened on the other side of campus.
I was nowhere near it.

Okay, I'm going to try to get
some sleep. I didn't even mention the

ash. It's everywhere, but I'm
guessing you know that all too well.
     I love you,
     F.

Text message from: Dad

On our way!

Text messages from: Felicia

Where are you?
Dad? Mom? RUOK?
Dad????

Subject: Your text

     I got your text! I haven't been
charging my phone much, so I don't

know when you sent it. I mean, the timestamp was current, but maybe it took a long time to get here, so I really don't know what's happening. It's driving me crazy.

Where are you? Are you almost here? Why can't you write back?

I went to the caff, got breakfast, and came back. Maybe you got cell service and sent the quickest message you could? I dunno.

Please be okay. Please.

Felicia

Subject: **The Dark**

So, this is bleak. The ash is two inches deep in most places. It's like snow that won't go away. The ash is toxic. Swell. Eventually, it will rain here, and that will only make a new sort of toxic mud mix everywhere. Hooray.

There's talk about how this will be horrific for all the grain crops, hell, all the crops everywhere in the Midwest. That's like most of our food, and who knows what has happened to the crops on the West Coast? Reports from there are spotty. Some locations did alright, but water up and down the coast is tainted with the ash so people are rationing. That's what we know from forwarded reports coming from the UK when we get news from London and New York. Chicago is under even more ash than we are. We've had some reports from there about what has happened to the Northwest and it's so horrible, I can't read it. Food relief is now coming from South America, Europe, and China to the United States. People are worried about invasion, but apparently, the President says we still have enough of a nuclear deterrence to prevent that from happening.

On the plus side, if there can be a plus side, global temperatures are down one degree Celsius and falling. Now that winter has come, it will be with us for at least the next several years, so we can expect another mini ice age. Global warming is solved! Well, not really, because The Dark may only last twenty to thirty years. Only twenty, you say? Is that a good thing or a bad thing? Well, it's bad news either way (did I say this was on the plus side?)

because we will be burning more
carbon to heat our homes than ever
before, and solar is now useless. Add
the lack of crops, and starvation
will soon be stalking the land a la
the fourteenth century (not the
twelfth, I looked it up). Unlike
solar, wind power is still working,
but all the effort that went into
preventing climate change is now
focused on surviving the fallout from
the eruption.

I've been spending a ton of time
in the library reading about the
little ice age that took place after
a massive (but not mega-colossal)
series of eruptions starting in the
thirteen hundreds. Good for glaciers,
good for polar bears (hooray!), and
very bad for humans.

So, as if we didn't know it
already, this will be bad.

The Ag-majors who stayed on
campus have recruited us to build
some indoor farms and to publish our
findings. It's slow going. Some
things work, some don't. Large-scale
wheat and corn are out of the
question. We have to focus on getting
the maximum nutrition from the
smallest possible footprint. Lots of
peas and potatoes. Ugh. It still
leaves us with the water problem, but

eventually, we'll have ice melt. Fingers crossed on that.

So, obviously, I'm keeping busy. I haven't written to you lately because, frankly, I gave up on ever seeing you again. I hit a bad depression, and if it weren't for this community, I can only guess what would have happened to me. The work has been a good way to keep my body moving, even if my mind is full of darkness. Did I quiet the darkness?

It's as if the sun has retreated from Ohio. We still see it, but it's dim. It's like I'm wearing Ray-Bans I can never take off. Even in winter, I miss the full warmth of the sun. I hope to live long enough to feel it on my face again. Remember tanning? I want to get a sunburn so bad, I can taste it. Turns out human beings need sunshine to produce vitamin D. Deb, one of the Bio-majors told me about it. We're all constantly sniffling and coughing from one flu or cold or another virus all the time now. More goddam Yellowstone effect. Hoorah.

So look, all things considered, I'm surviving. I work on the hothouses during the day and do some patrols in the evening. I know my way around a long gun. Thankfully, we've got that part handled. No attacks in a while, but we're ready for them if they start up again. I have no empathy for those freaks. They had their chance to join up. It's too late now.

Anyway, it's late. Pitch black, with a dim half moon and a couple of stars. Not a cloud in the sky today except the freaking Yellowstone cloud, and that's always there.

F.

Subject: Posterity

If you're reading these emails, I hope you are safe and well, and the world is returning or has returned to its former friendly abundance. Don't make the same mistakes we did. Don't fall back into the stupid habit of burning all the carbon you can find, tempting as that may be. Don't assume everything will stay rosy and bright. Read our accounts, read your history. You don't have to suffer the way low-tech civilizations did when the earth coughed up a moon-sized chunk of lava and blanketed the atmosphere with dust. Also, don't create a new catastrophe by blowing smoke into the sky. You can't put a price on a habitable environment. Science can't fix everything, but it can help us prevent the preventable and prepare for the inevitable. Study, learn, and be ready.

And don't give up hope!

Only a week after the last email in my chain (Subject: The Dark), my family arrived at my dorm room in Oberlin in that crazy electric truck they bought in Fargo. Their impossible journey is documented by my sister (see Our Post-Apocalyptic Road Trip by Sunny Thompson in these archives). All I can say about our reunion is that we cried for a week straight, even my dad.

Our government finally got their act together to send some help, but more importantly, it linked us with other communities of scholars working on the means to survive this mess. You have your food and water rations thanks to their concerted efforts. Remember that people can do better by working together. Let me repeat that. People do better by working together. Make it a mantra.

Thank you to the Library of Congress for collecting our stories

for future generations.
Stay safe, love your neighbors,
be vigilant, and do better TOGETHER.

All my love,
Felicia Thompson, Bethlehem, PA,
October 18, year 5AY

Lincoln, Nebraska

Judy

by Lisa Orban

Day 7???

It's been a week since the emergency broadcast warned everyone to take immediate shelter from Yellowstone exploding. At least, I think it's been a week, honestly, it's kinda hard to tell anymore. I've been holed up in my bathroom and the frosted glass window doesn't really give off a lot of light and time is blurring the longer I stay here.

When it first started, I almost ignored my phone when it started blaring. I thought it was probably something stupid like a broadcast test, not an actual emergency. But then it started talking about Yellowstone erupting and that it was bad and we were in the danger zone, and to shelter in place, with warnings about the dangers of falling ash and not to try to drive through it because it could stall cars and breathing it could kill you. They said to find a room that you could seal up from ash and to wait for emergency services. So, that's what I did.

I couldn't think of anywhere but my bathroom, since the window is sealed shut and I could cover the vent and the push a towel under the door. I started throwing things in as fast as I could from all over the apartment and I've spent the last couple of days sorting through everything, and that's how I found this notebook. At first I was using it for inventory, but then I decided to start using it as a journal until help comes. I don't have anything better to do.

I tried calling Mom and Dad, but they didn't answer. They live in Denver and I'm really worried about them. If it's this bad here, it has to be worse there. I kept trying to call until the phone stopped working, that was a few days ago and now it's dead. The power went out not long after the announcement. I still have running water, sort of anyway, but it's starting to look kinda grey now. I filled the bathtub with water once I cleared it out, and I can still flush the toilet (thank god!) but I'm not sure for how much longer.

The ash keeps building up in the window. It looks like a really dirty snowstorm outside. I hope it doesn't completely cover the window. I found my hand-cranked camp light in my camping stuff that I threw in here and I keep lighting it up and putting it in the window hoping someone will see it and come for me. It's not very bright, but it's the only thing I could think of to let people know I'm here.

I wish I had more room to stretch out. The bathroom was easy to seal up, and it seemed like a good idea, but after 7??? days couped up in this small space, I think I might be losing my mind a little. With all my stuff in here it feels even smaller than it actually is. I've got my sleeping bag up against the door and I can look out of the window from here, not that there's anything too look at just a grey blob of light during the day, and even less than that at night.

I wonder how my friends are doing. Did they try to get out or did they do like me and hole up in their rooms? I'm not that far from the university, and I thought about trying to make it over there, but I don't know if I should. The emergency message said to shelter in place and I'm not even sure if I could get in, they might have the doors locked.

I tried calling after I sealed myself into the bathroom but all I could get was busy signals. And when I tried to Facetime it would just make the connecting sound but it wouldn't connect with anyone. I tried sending out text messages to everyone but I never got anything back. I don't know why nothing works and it's weird not knowing what's going on in the world.

Before my phone died, I couldn't connect with anything. Just a big nothing. No messages or notifications of any kind. I've never felt so alone. I've never been without a phone since I was a kid. Hell, I haven't written on paper since… since, god I don't even know anymore. Grade school maybe? Who needed paper when you had a phone or laptop? Even all my schoolwork was sent in from my computer to my teachers.

And now, here I am, all alone, writing into a notebook like one of those characters from a disaster book. My life has become a disaster story! Okay… this is just stupid. I'm not some rando character from a stupid book, I'm a real person and I don't like this at all. I don't like being alone and not knowing what to do. Why couldn't I have had friends over when this happened? Or been out where the people were when this happened? Why did I have to tell everyone I was staying in to work on that stupid paper instead of hanging out with my friends?

I thought moving out of the dorms and getting this apartment off campus was a great idea at the beginning of this semester, but now I wish I had stayed. At least then I would have had other people around me and I wouldn't be stuck in a 4x6 bathroom all by myself.

I'm going to sleep for awhile. I hope someone comes soon.

Day 8

Well, no one has come yet, so I guess I'll keep writing. It's really quiet outside. No birds or traffic or anything, it's really creepy and I don't like it. I think I hear my neighbors every once in a while but when I yell no one answers and I don't want to leave to go look. I do hear the building creaking, and it worries me. How heavy is ash? More than snow? Less than snow? Could the roof cave in? I wish I knew…

Well, on the bright side, I have 2 cases of bottled water and I remembered to throw in my can opener. I did forget silverware, so I'm eating everything with my fingers, but at least I can get into the cans. I've taken a full inventory of all the food and if I'm really careful, I can probably make it about 2 weeks... maybe. I'm allowing myself 2 bottles of water a day, one for drinking and the other for making food. I don't really recommend cold soup, but it's better than nothing.

Some of the stuff I threw in here I can't do anything with. Rice, romen, noddles, things like that all need heat of some kind and I don't have anyway of heating things.

Speaking of heating things, it's starting to get colder. I'm not sure if it's because of the ash covering the sky or just because it's fall and the weather is unpredictable, but it's definitely getting colder. Thank god I remembered to throw in my sleeping bag and pillows or I'd really be miserable. I've made a nest of all my blankets and pillows next to the door and it's not too bad for sleeping. I wish my bathroom was bigger, with all the stuff I have in here, there's not a lot of room to move around and I have stuff stacked up everywhere. Last night I about scared myself to death when I kicked over my tower of canned goods in front of the sink in my sleep. So, I moved those this morning to the other side of the sink so I don't do that again. One can hit me on my ankle and it's bruised today but I don't think it's anything more than a bruise, at least that's what I'm hoping anyway.

If I'm right about the days, it's Saturday today. If this hadn't happened I'd be at Angie's birthday party with all my friends. We'd have gone out to dinner together, probably pizza, and then a few stops at our favorite places to drink and sing karaoke, and who knows, maybe there'd even be cake. I'm sure we would have had cake and we would have sang happy birthday to her and did all that stuff.

I guess, on the bright side, I don't have to worry about that term paper I've been stressed out about now. It was due on Monday, and I hadn't finished it. I was planning on having it done before the party, even if I had to stay up all night on Friday to get it done.

It's weird to think of all the undone things that were the focus of my life just a few days ago. The pile of laundry I had taken to the laundrymat, but hadn't put away that I kept scolding myself over. The grocery shopping I was supposed to do but kept putting off. The homework I was working on when the announcement started. All the plans I had with my friends and the trip I had planned with my parents during winter break.

Nothing is ever going to be the same again. Everything is turned upside down and I don't know what's going to happen. I keep hoping someone finds me soon, but every day that hope gets smaller. Does anyone even know to look for me? If my friends were rescued, they'd let them know I was here, right? They wouldn't forget about me, would they? Someone has to come for me, right? That's how it works. There's an emergency, and then they declare it a disaster and they send out FEMA, and the Salvation Army and the national guard to find and help people. That's how it's **supposed** to work. I just wait here and someone finds me, because in an emergency it's better to wait where people can find you rather than just wandering away. Right? Those are the rules, when something bad happens you stop and you wait for rescue.

But, what if they don't?

No! They'll come for me. The have to come for me. The radio said to shelter in place and to wait for rescue. That's what they said and that's what I'm doing.

Okay, I have to stop. I need to calm down and think positive thoughts. Panic isn't going to help. I have food, and water, and I'm safe, and when someone comes they'll be able to find me because of the light I keep in the window and they'll know I'm here and they'll take me to safety and everything will be okay.

I'm going to stop writing and make something to eat and then try to get some more sleep.

Day 9

Hello again. Still stuck in the bathroom. I'm getting restless. I wish there was something I could do but mostly I just sit here and stare out the window or sleep. Once a day I turn on my battery powered radio to listen to see if anyone is out there, but it's just static. I only listen for 15 minutes at a time because I don't have many batteries for it. I found it when I was going through my camping bag. Along with the radio and light, I found matches, this notebook, a cast-iron skillet, some twine, clothes pins, and a few other odds & ends I keep in my bag.

My parents and I were planning our yearly ski trip for Christmas before everything went to shit. As cold as it's getting, I've been thinking about sneaking out of here and grabbing my parka, maybe even my snow boots. I left all of that in the closet when I was pitching stuff into the bathroom, but it's getting more tempting to leave and see what it really looks like outside and maybe grab a few other things I might need.

I don't know if I should. There's no ash in here and I do have blankets, food, light, and the radio. If I leave, would I be bringing that back in here with me? Is it worth it? I mean, someone could show up at any time and find me, so why take the risk? But, what if no one comes? What then? Am I going to die in my bathroom???

I thought I was so grown up moving so far away from home, but I miss mom and dad. I really wish they were here with me. They'd know what to do and I wouldn't be so alone. The silence is killing me. It's like I'm the only thing left alive. I don't like it and I want to go home or wake up tomorrow in my bed with all of this nothing but a bad dream.

But every night, I lay down to sleep and I wake up to this. Crying doesn't help, but here I am, crying again and I can't stop. Please, somebody fine me. I don't want to be alone anymore.

Day 10

I heard a low rumbling sound earlier today and for a minute I got excited thinking maybe it was a truck. But then I realized it was a storm coming. The rain started about an hour ago and it's cleared some of the ash from the window, but the glass has more of a grey look to it than it did before. I heard somewhere that wet ash turns into something like concrete and now I'm really worried. I don't know for sure how much has fallen, but there were at least 6 inches of ash piling up in the window before it started raining. Now it's more like 2 inches, but it's darker than it was before.

I've been hearing more creaking and popping above me since the rain started. I'm really getting worried. I think the roof might collapse. I'm on the first floor, but what happens if it falls in? I might??? be okay??? For a little bit anyway, but I'm not sure how much longer I can stay here. It's been almost 2 weeks since it started, and I haven't heard emergency vehicles or anything else. Just the sounds of my roof popping and creaking, static from the radio and now the storm. What's happening out there? Why isn't anyone coming for me? For anyone? Where is everyone? I can't be the only person left, could I???

I'm getting scared. Really scared.

Day 11

The storm stopped sometime during the night. I can hear water dripping outside my window, but it's no brighter than it was the day before. I turned my radio on this morning, but it died after about 10 minutes. I have one set of batteries left but I'm going to save them for tomorrow.

My ankle is all purple today and it hurts when I rotate it. Stupid can! But, I've been propping it up hoping that will help. I found Tylenol in medicine cabinet and took some. It's helped a little bit. I also found my first aid kit under the sink and it had an ice pack in it, but I'm saving that for just in case. I can only use it once, and I might need it for something else later. Maybe I'm being too cautious, but I don't know how long I'm going to be stuck here and what if something worse happens?

The water in the bathtub is starting to get an ick to

it. I definitely don't want to drink it, but I can still use it for the toilet. Which is good since it stopped refilling sometime after the storm. How awful would it be if I couldn't flush the toilet??? That may be the only good thing about picking this tiny assed room to hole up in!

I'm really starting to feel claustrophobic right now. I haven't been able to move around more than a few steps for two weeks. I need to move, but there's nowhere to move to. Five steps long and 3 steps wide is all I have and that's while picking my way around all this stuff.

I've been pushing the empty cans and containers behind the toilet, and as far away as I can from where I'm sleeping, but that pile is starting to get bigger than full stuff. I've eaten more food than I have left. Most of the water bottles still have water in them but that's only because I was refilling them from the sink until the water stopped. I'm not going to drink it if I can help it since it all has sediment at that bottom once the water settles. But I figured I could use it to wash myself and if I run out of tub water for the toilet, I can use those instead for a little bit.

I need a plan. I can't stay here much longer.

Day 12

I think the neighbors roof caved in today. I was staring out the window when I heard a loud popping noise and then a loud, long crash. I climbed up on the sink to get a better look out the window, but it was hard to tell if that's what happened. But, the house does seem shorter.

I didn't hear any screams or see anything move

outside. I can't see much, but I'm sure I'd be able to see at least blobs moving around outside. I guess they weren't home when it happened or maybe they left as soon as they heard the news. I was so busy trying to throw stuff into the bathroom I didn't even look outside to see what anyone else was doing. I think that was a mistake. Maybe I should have tried to leave or found someone to hide with. I should have run to the campus and found help there. But, I didn't think it would be like this, I thought they'd send help in a day or two after things started to settle and now I'm just here all by myself.

I've decided I need to leave. I can't get trapped here if the same happens to my apartment building. I've been thinking about all the ski equipment I have and maybe I could ski out of here. I know it sounds stupid, but ash has got to be sorta like snow, right? I've been skiing since I was a kid, and my ankle isn't hurting as much today. If I wait a few more days, it should be completely healed and I can try anyway.

I could probably make it 10, maybe 15 miles a day on my ski's. Depending on what the ash is like anyway. I'm not the best cross-country skier, but I'm not bad either. But, the real question is, where do I go if I leave? And should I follow the highways or try to strike out in a straight line instead? I think the highway might make for smoother skiing, and I'm more likely to find someone if I do but going cross-country I could, in theory, put more miles between me and here each day.

But, I don't know where to go honestly. I think my best option is to head generally east. I need a map to plan this out and I have one... in my closet... I just need to be able to get to it.

So, I think tomorrow I'm going to try and make a mask to cover my face, push everything away from the door and cover it with one of my blankets, and then venture out and see what I can find. Maybe even look out the windows and see what it really looks like outside.

Day 13

Well, that was awful! I did get what I needed and found a few more helpful things, but everything outside of my apartment is just horrifying. And I'm thinking of going out in it! What am I thinking?! At least I'm safe in the bathroom. Honestly, as long as I'm careful I could probably venture out into my apartment whenever I needed to.

I closed all the windows and locked my doors before holing up in the bathroom, so it's not terrible out there. There's fine layer of ash settled on things, but it's not thick. It probably came up through the vents. If I'm careful, like I was today, I don't kick very much of it up.

But outside looks like a wasteland. Everything is covered in ash and it's all grey and lifeless. I saw the neighbor's dog when I was looking out the back windows. I don' t know why he was outside or why they left him, but I about cried when I saw Charlie laying dead in the yard. He was such a good dog, why would they leave him trapped on his lead like that? If I had known, I would have brought him inside with me. What if I leave here and I end up like Charlie? Dead, on the side of the road, with no one to help me or find me?

Oh god, what am I going to do???

Day 14

I still don't know what the right thing to do is. I've been looking over the map, and if I do this, I could take I-80 up to Omaha and then over to Des Moines and that will take me straight over to the Mississippi. But that's over 300 miles away. A month, traveling in this, if I can do 10 miles a day, every day.

Could I do that?

It's possible that I could find help before that, maybe. But, I don't know. The radio is still nothing but static, no matter how much I go up and down the dial. But I can't be the only living thing left in the world, could I? No! That's just stupid. There has to be more people out there, it couldn't have blanketed the entire world. Could it?

But, I need to decide very soon. I found a few more things to eat when I went out yesterday, but not a lot. A bag of chips, a box a saltines, a few other things that were still in sealed packages. I didn't even want to open the refrigerator but I was able to find a little more to eat. But no more water. But, I did find a 2 liter bottle of soda tucked into a corner in the pantry.

But, right now my choices are wait here and try to stretch my food out as long as possible while I wait for rescue and hope my ceiling doesn't fall down on top of me like the neighbors did the other day. Or, I can pack up what I can carry in my backpack and head out on my ski's and hope for the best.

Neither one is a great option. But, if I'm going to leave, I should do it soon.

I know if Dad was here he'd have a plan. He was always great when we went camping, bragging about being a boy scout and all the badges he earned when he was in high school and trying to teach me everything he knew about wilderness training. Now I'm racking my brain trying to remember everything he tried to teach me. I should have listened better, but I didn't think I was ever going to need it. Why would I?

Whenever we went camping there was always other people around, and cell phones, and park rangers, and civilization never that far away. I never took what he said seriously. I liked spending time with him and camping was always a fun time, but it was just that, fun. I didn't think the things he was trying to teach me meant anything except as an excuse for us to spent time together.

I'm sorry Dad. I really should have listened better when you took us camping and I promise if I get out of this and see you again I'll let you were right all along. This was important to learn, I was just too stupid to know it.

Day 15

Okay, I'm leaving tomorrow. I heard a loud crack above me that shook the apartment building. I left the bathroom to go look after the shaking stopped and halfway up the outside hallway, I saw sky. I can't stay here much longer. I'm lucky that it was only a bed-sized hole, but ash is swirling around and it won't take much to start filling up the hallway.

While I was out, I went ahead and packed up all my skiing equipment and brought it to the bathroom. It's really crowded in here now but I won't be here much longer. Now I just need to decide what to take and what to leave behind.

I want to take everything, but the weight will slow me down. So, I think it's mostly going to be food, but I have to be careful because cans are heavy, and I need water more than canned goods. If I stick to 10 water bottles, and all the packaged food like crackers, cereal, poptarts, and things like that that don't weigh as much, I think I'll be okay. They aren't the healthiest things I could pick, but they are all sealed and won't weigh me down too much. And I'm sure I'll be able to find food along way, at least, that's my hope.

I also need my first aid kit, and I should grab some extra stuff to pack in there from the medicine cabinet. God knows, if I'm going to try to do 10 miles a day in this I'm going to need the Tylenol. I'm going to be aching trying to keep that pace, but what choice do I have?

I have my ski mask, but I don't know if that will be enough to keep the ash out. But, if I wear my parka completely zipped up and my knitted ski mask over it, maybe that will be? I hope so. Because I don't have anything else right now.

On my way out of town, I might stop and see what I can find at the hardware store. Maybe the have N95 masks or something else I can use. I do have my small camping hatchet that I plan on bringing with me, I also have my sleeping bag and tent. They all fit on my backpack frame, so they won't take up any space that I need for food/water.

I guess it's a good thing I grew up in a family that

liked outdoor activities like camping and skiing. At least I have a chance at this because of it.

I'm really scared but I have to do this. I can't stay here any longer. No one is coming for me and I'm going to have to try and save myself. With any luck, I'll find people, or they'll find me. My ski suit is bright pink, so I should stand out from the rest of the grey background if anyone's looking for survivors.

I've decided to take the highway route. If I stick to where people should be, it will be easier to find me and less chance of getting lost if I go cross-country. I don't want to get turned around and start going in circles with no landmarks to help me find my way.

I'm scared to leave, but if I don't go now I'll run out of food and water and then I won't be able to do anything but die, alone, in this stupid bathroom. I don't want to die, trapped in here like a wounded animal. My dad would be so disappointed in me if I did that. He raised me to take care of myself, and now I'm going to try and make him proud of me and get myself out of here and to safety.

And who knows, maybe once I make it to my cousin's house, she'll know where my parents are. I know, the chances of them being anywhere but dead are small, but if anyone could make it out alive, it's Dad. I have to keep hoping that I'll see Mom and Dad again because I can't think about a world without them right now. Everything is too much already and I just can't let myself give into the fear that's been with me since this whole thing started.

And who knows, maybe once I'm out of my apartment, I'll get picked up right away. I mean, the university isn't far away and if they were going to set up a disaster staging area, that would be a good location for it. I'm going to swing by the campus on my way out of town and see if I can find anyone but if not, I'll head straight out of town following the route I picked.

I have to believe there are people out there and that I'll be able to find them. Or better yet, rescue finds me and takes me to safety. But, I'm young, and strong, and I've been an active outdoor person my whole life. I've won cross-country races when I was younger and I can do this. I have to do this.

So, I'm going to try and eat until I'm completely full from the food I'm not going to be able to take with and then try and get a good night's sleep and be rested in the morning. It may be my last chance to sleep comfortably – well, as comfortably as you can in a tiny bathroom anyway.

Then in the morning, I'm going to use the last of my water that I'm not taking with me to get clean and put on clean clothes. If I need more clothes, I'm sure I'll be able to find some along the way. It's not like anyone is watching the stores anymore. I hope I can find food along the way. I know that's what people panic buy whenever there's bad weather, but I don't think people had enough time to that this time.

I'll try and finish what I have from the discard food pile before I leave. I can't take it and it's stupid to let it go to waste, and I know how hungry I'll get from skiing. It takes a lot to keep going, but it will be faster, and probably safer than walking on this stuff.

On the bright side, while it's getting cold, it's not like standing on top of a mountain cold. So, maybe it won't be so bad. At least I won't freeze to death.

Okay, this is it. My last night here. Tomorrow I will leave and whatever happens, at least I know I tried my best and I didn't give up.

Day 16

Well, everything is packed and ready to leave. I decided I wasn't going to take this journal with me. I didn't want to lose any extra space I might need and I can't imagine that I'll have any time to write in it once I leave.

If anyone does find this, I'll be traveling on I-80 heading first to Omaha, then on to Des Moines - Iowa City - Davenport into Illinois in a bright pink parka. I have a cousin that lives in Springfield, and while we've never been close, I can't think of anywhere else to go. I hope that I will find people before that, please let me find people before that! - but if you are my would-be rescuer, that's the route I'm taking and if you can send someone to find me I would be forever grateful.

Judy

Chihuahuan Desert, Arizona

Chet Davis

by Timothy R. Baldwin

1

The lights flickered to the rhythm of metal-on-metal clanging above where I crouched in an access tunnel. Overhead, hidden in the ductwork, I had stashed away items in case of an emergency. I didn't trust the system we all relied upon, with good reason — I knew it intimately. More clanging came, and I ticked off the last set of dashes and dots and closed my notebook. Now was not the time to emerge. Not yet, anyway.

Those who had made it underground still mourned the loss of those millions who wouldn't. I thank God for our survival, and now the fate of humanity rests with us. The food supply wasn't enough to sustain more than the few hundred souls who had made it below. I doubted the Surface Dwellers who survived the Great Eruption above fared much better.

The survivors below were my responsibility; I had to protect them from the violence brooding underground, threatening to explode at any moment.

Every day some scuffle caught the attention of Governor Ortiz, the leader of this underground ark. An otherwise peaceful community might soon become an inescapable city prison where every person fended for their own. Ortiz spoke of a police state in his last briefing, but for now, we must maintain the status quo: monitor access points, maintain the HVAC and water treatment systems, and ration food supplies.

My radio crackled. "Davis, we've got some unusual readings in mechanical room Zone Five."

I doubted they needed me. Still, I had to see for myself. "I'm on my way."

I climbed through the access panel beneath me and reached up to shut and lock the door. Another few steps down the ladder and from the catwalk in Zone One, I glanced up at the access door. The clanging had stopped for now. This time tomorrow, it will likely pick up again. I imagined some poor sap trudging through several inches of volcanic ash to pound out a message to an anonymous recipient. The pounding had begun during one of my shifts and continued regularly after that. I doubted this was a coincidental correspondence. Instead, someone outside knew of my existence and expected me to keep their communications secret. While the other bunkers reported improved air quality and new plant growth, this one-way correspondence via

Morse code reported far more bleak news.

The government, now stationed on the coastal perimeters where they received only a dusting of ash, intended to keep people underground for as long as possible. Its agencies insisted humanity's survival depended on all nine bunkers, with Bunker Nine as the focal point.

The construction of these nine bunkers had been extensive and costly. Not all involved in the development had opted to squirrel themselves underground. Others volunteered to stay above ground as a sustainable network of proverbial doves to seek out inhabitable land beyond the scorched earth above us. Reports came in daily from the other eight bunkers from East to West throughout the United States. For those regions that survived, volcanic ash and air toxicity still made much of the U.S. uninhabitable. The people of Bunker Nine accepted their fate: safety and security with the promise of a better tomorrow for their children.

I wondered if they would be so willing if they knew the truth. Six months ago, Bunker Nine's true purpose progressively revealed itself when the knocking began. Phase One would begin, and I waited for the signal.

My footsteps echoed on the catwalk as I passed through a corridor leading to Zone Two. I nodded to Gary, one of the uniformed guards on patrol during my shift.

Gary nodded back. "How're things in the mechanical room?"

"Everything is copacetic," I told him.

"Have the pipes been fixed?"

His question referred to the banging on the surface. Until now, I'd convinced Gary the noise was due to knocking pipes.

"It's not an issue," I said, repeating this exchange almost verbatim from previous days. "Besides, it only happens at night when the surface is likely cooling."

Gary nodded. "I had a thought, though. What if there were survivors? What if they found our bunker and tried to get in?"

I waved him off. "Rumors and bedtime stories."

Gary chuckled. "You're right. Surface Dwellers. Poor S.O.B.S. They should've prepared as we did."

Ignoring his comment, I hurried on. He didn't have a clue. No one could have truly prepared for that day. Heck! Gary and most of us below ground couldn't have prepared. Not on our own, anyway. We worked with the government and the corporations that funded this extensive project.

As a steamfitter and a damn good one, like everyone else below ground, the right people employed me. I oversaw the construction of the entire HVAC system in this underground ark. No one else knew their way around the maze of pipes and wires that cooled and heated everything and everybody, ensuring our continued survival. Fortunately, I had been able to take my family below just before devastation hit. Limited space didn't allow for extended family members, and telling them about the bunker would have risked humanity's continued survival.

Still, we could've reduced the deaths. With more time and resources, we could have saved everyone. People could have even prepared on their own. But the eruption came upon us quicker than expected. And just as suddenly, we quietly herded underground.

We'd built this bunker beneath the Chihuahuan Desert in Arizona, well over one thousand miles south of Yellowstone. Even at this distance, the layers of ash and the toxicity in the air made the surface uninhabitable. The survivors banged daily on the reinforced steel in Zone One. Some chalked the daily banging up to desperation, but the rhythmic nature of the knocking and its timing implied a code. I knew of no other inside man or woman within the bunker working with me.

Rumors about a coup spread throughout the bunker. Governor Ortiz responded by forming a quasi-task force, but most — including Ortiz — believed a coup unlikely. Finding no new information and being unable to corroborate a single rumor, the task force quickly dissolved. But without doubt, someone with enough tenacity and explosives would be able to break through our little fortress. The survivors hadn't found the other access points, and they wouldn't be able to tap into our air and water supply. The atmosphere and water would recycle in this self-contained, self-sustaining bunker for the next hundred years. We'd likely run out of food before the recycling systems, and CO_2 scrubbers failed.

The bunker contained three levels and five zones. Zones Three through Five held residential apartments, no larger than 320 square feet. A family of four had enough room to sleep comfortably in two separate bedrooms but not enough room to spend every waking hour together. My family lived in Zone Four, just above the commissary, the mess hall, and the recreation facility. Zone One housed operations, communications, and command, while Zone Two housed the main facilities and operations. Each zone had its own mechanical rooms, which communicated with operations.

With lights out for the night, the bunker resonated with a gentle, mechanical hum. I nodded as I passed each guard patrolling the zones in upper-level catwalks. With brief longing, I passed above the apartment where my wife, teenage daughter, and son slept soundly for the night. My wife and I had caught our daughter and son once or twice sneaking out for some shenanigans with a handful of other teens, but a mandatory curfew in response to lingering fears of a coup squelched any further attempts at sneaking out.

At the catwalk access door leading to Zone Five, I spun the wheel, and the door opened with a hiss. The temperature in Zone Five was noticeably warmer. Yet, a cool draft passed through the garage-sized opening between Zone Four and Five, thus maintaining a steady circulation of air, which Zone Five didn't reciprocate.

I hit the call button on the radio strapped to my shoulder. "Davis to Operations. What are the temperature readings in Zone Five?"

"Seventy-Eight."

Not alarming, but higher than the preferred seventy-two. "Is it holding?"

"It's been rising one degree every hour. Jacobs and Matthews are working on it in the mechanical room."

"Jacobs and Matthews?" I asked. "They're not on the schedule for tonight."

"They volunteered for overtime."

Those guys never volunteered for anything. They were up to something. I picked up the pace and passed over more residential apartments. Sweat beaded on my brow: the temperature had to be well over eighty.

Like Zone One, this mechanical room was located on the farthest side of Zone Five and well away from the residences. Any problems with the HVAC would immediately impact the closest residents. By now, their apartments had to be sweatboxes.

As if to confirm my suspicions, an apartment door opened below me.

A woman spoke. "Is that better?"

A muffled voice answered, and the woman shuffled around for a moment before retreating into her apartment. The door remained open.

I continued until I came to the access door to Zone Five's mechanical room, where I reached for the handle and recoiled from the heat.

I radioed operations. "Operations. Code Red. We've got a fire in Zone Five."

Sirens sounded, and red lights flashed. They executed the drill – a quick evacuation to the neighboring zone. I didn't have much time before the seal would close over Zone Five. I turned and raced down the catwalk toward Zone Four. The computerized countdown to total lockdown had already sounded over the speakers, and people had begun the evacuation.

Thirty-eight seconds.

Support beams started to buckle.

Thirty seconds.

The mechanical room door blew off its hinges; heat roared toward my backside.

Eighteen seconds.

The bunker groaned and screamed.

Ten seconds.

Gears activated. Who else faced incineration once we were locked inside?

Two seconds.

I dove through the closing access door as flames leaped toward the remaining gap in the door. The door slammed with a resounding thud and bolted tight.

Panicked voices called out for loved ones. Residents of Zone Four joined in the search and rescue. It wouldn't take long for the rest of the bunker's residences to understand there had been a fire. Security was already on its way to assist in relocation.

My radio crackled. "Davis. Report to Bunker Command."

As the overseer of the HVAC project, I would be the subject of scrutiny. I grasped for a plausible explanation as I headed to Bunker Command.

2

A video played. Jacobs and Matthews diligently worked on the HVAC units. Three hours in, we'd found nothing.

Governor Ortiz sat beside me. "Still nothing?"

"Nothing."

Ortiz asked the same question every hour, and I gave him the same reply. I requested a break, and Ortiz nodded to the operator, who paused the film. The governor stood and stretched.

"Chet, I have complete faith in you. If there's an

anomaly, you'll find it."

"And if there isn't?"

His eyes locked on mine. "We'll cross that bridge when we get there." Ortiz cleared his throat. "If you'll excuse me, relocation plans need authorization."

Ortiz departed, and the operator allowed a five-minute recess. When I returned, Major Dixon, our head of security, had taken the governor's chair. He invited me to sit. I opted to stand.

"Play the reel."

The operator nodded and flipped a switch. Jacobs and Matthews moved between pieces of equipment. One knelt, another stood, while the other fiddled with a control panel. Another hour passed like this.

"There!" I saw the spark.

The operator paused the reel, and Dixon narrowed his eyes and drew closer to the screen. "Sabotage? Faulty equipment?"

I shook my head. "A thorough investigation is impossible until the unit cools."

Dixon stood, and his steely-eyed glare softened before he spoke. "Be with your family. Get your rest. It'll be a long time before you can do anything like that again."

What that implied, I had no idea. Had Ortiz already decided my fate? Even if he had, it wouldn't be prudent to bring a member of security, the head or otherwise, in on a decision before further evidence surfaced. Though I hadn't been arrested, I heeded Dixon's advice. I headed home.

3

Unescorted as I trekked toward Zone Four, I breathed more freely. Glad of the silence, broken only by my footfalls, I put distance between myself and command.

My family awaited, likely with a bombardment of questions. But what would I tell them? There was an explosion in Zone Five. They already knew that.

The door to my unit opened, and my wife, Alena, stood before me. "What'll happen next?"

"No idea."

Samantha and Jordan joined her in the living room, daughter and son flanking her.

I met Samantha's eyes, then Jordan's eyes. "Am I not allowed in?"

"I told you he wouldn't tell us anything." Samantha huffed and stomped away. Alena smirked as she stepped toward me. "Sam's just worried about Nick. Since the explosion, she hasn't heard from him."

I wrapped my arms around Alena and kissed her. "We didn't lose any families housed in Zone Five," I spoke louder. "Sam, you don't have to worry about Nick and his family. They're just being relocated."

Jordan spoke. "Dad, what aren't you telling us?"

I gazed into Alena's eyes, then stepped away. Sam had rejoined us and leaned with her arms crossed against the wall.

"Nothing we can share at this moment. Trust me, okay?"

Alena turned away from me and addressed Samantha and Jordan. "Dinner is in fifteen. Go finish your studies."

Sam began to protest. "We already—"

"Listen to your mother," I said, plopping myself upon the couch.

With a grumble, they walked away. Jordan cursed, then closed the bedroom door behind him. Sam glared at me, her eyes wide, then marched out of the front door and slammed it. Alena wrung her hands and sighed. "They can't handle being underground much longer."

I chewed my bottom lip. I wouldn't give voice to my agreement. "Getting out too soon will expose us to all kinds of toxins."

Alena sat. "Chet, things are set in motion now."

I nodded and whispered. "Not here, and not out loud."

She pulled back. "Do you think they suffered much?"

"Doubtful," I said.

I locked eyes with hers. Alena simultaneously shrank back and rose to her feet. She forced a smile. "How about a drink?"

I didn't answer, but she got the hint. Alena turned her back to me and disappeared into the kitchen. A cupboard door creaked open, the water turned on for a moment, turned off, and the microwave beeped four times before humming to life.

The sound gave voice to an image playing in my mind of two men, both of whom I hired and trained personally. Matthews, the younger, had a child on the way, while Jacobs, just a few years older than me, had already seen his kids off to college just before the eruption. Matthews wouldn't live to see his child grow up in a world of ash and toxins, while Jacobs would no longer mourn the children he'd been unable to save.

It should've been me in the mechanical room, the first to inhale the fumes, which would've swept me away in a dreamless sleep. Like Mathews and Jacobs, the flames would've consumed me with no time for my nerve endings to register pain. Alena would've understood. My children, not so much.

Alena returned and handed me a cup of tea. Steam rose from the mug, and I allowed its heat to warm my hands. I took a sip.

She sat. "Have they given you any further instruction?"

The ominous *They*. Not Ortiz and his skeleton of a government, and certainly not those in the bunker. The Surface Dwellers above — those who survived — didn't know me, my name, or what I had done. But a handful, a few hundred, and maybe even fewer than that, knew me. They'd recruited me and called themselves The Agency. In exchange for my coerced cooperation, they ensured my safety and that of my family if I did one small thing in the design. They called it an orchestrated flaw, one which marked the beginning of Phase One. Though today's explosion surprised me, I figured it was the sign The Agency told me to expect.

I set the tea down and met Alena's gaze. "They haven't communicated further instructions, and they wouldn't communicate that quickly. Besides, whatever comes next can't be done alone. There must be another operative on the inside. I'm sure of it."

Alena stood. "I'm sure it won't be long."

The front door opened, and Sam had a bounce in

her step as she entered. "I found Nick in the commissary."

"That's great, sweetheart," I said. "How are he and his family adjusting?"

Sam shrugged. "Okay, I guess. Mom, can I help you finish preparing dinner?"

Alena gave me a peck on the cheek, then my wife and daughter went into the kitchen.

I mourned the loss of my children's innocence. Parting ways with a boyfriend or girlfriend used to be a passing thing. But not now, not in the wake of an explosion within the safe confines of a bunker.

That was my doing, and soon I'd drag my family into a conflict long in the making.

4

Fragmented images of Jacobs's and Matthews's last moments plagued my dreams as I tossed and turned beside Alena that night.

They glanced at each other. Matthews said something, and Jacobs laughed in response. The spark appeared, bright and instantaneous. A ball of flame rose and expanded. It consumed the bodies of the two men. Neither had time to react or even writhe in agony as the fire engulfed the rest of the equipment. Then came the blast and flames licking at my back.

Alena shook me and cried out. "They're at the door."

Someone pounded on the door and shouted. "Open up!"

I recognized the muffled cadence of the voice.

"Stay here," I told Alena as I arose from the bed. The pounding continued. When I reached the front door, I glanced behind me and saw Samantha and Jordan peering through the darkness.

"Shut the door and go back to bed," I hissed.

Samantha stuck out her tongue and let the door close with a thud. I opened the front door. With bags under his eyes and stubble on his face, Major Dixon flashed me a thin smile and brushed past me.

"The council is digging into the circumstances surrounding your journey to Bunker Nine." Dixon sat and massaged his temples. "Do you have anything to drink around here?"

Alena chimed in. "I can make some tea."

Dixon waved her off. "Something stronger."

"We can't store liquor in our apartments," I said.

Dixon glanced at me and grinned. "Surely you smuggled in a stash."

I exchanged a glance with Alena and nodded. She retreated into the kitchen and flipped on the lights. I pulled up a seat across from Dixon and waited.

Why was the major really here? I couldn't consider him an ally or an adversary. Not yet, anyway. Until recently, my encounters with him consisted of listening to his security briefings in monthly meetings. Beyond that, our paths rarely crossed.

Dixon sat up and leaned toward me. "This bunker is a meticulously planned community. The creators spent trillions on designing every detail of it. The eight others arc cxact copies. After the explosion, communications between the other bunkers went down. We haven't been ablc to get them back up, but you know that already.

This facility was supposed to be flawless, and a security breach would have been impossible. Unless, of course, the breach occurred sometime during construction."

Alena returned with a tumbler containing a double shot of bourbon. Dixon thanked her as he took the glass. In one gulp, he downed it and placed it on the table between us.

He sighed. "Wonderful."

"Did you need anything else, Major?"

"Nothing," the major said. "Please, Alena, join us."

Alena and I exchanged a glance. While my nerves reeled, her face appeared expressionless.

He chuckled. "Sit back, Chet. Relax. I've got something to show you."

He reached into his pocket and produced a rectangular casing about the size of an engagement ring box. As he opened it, he displayed a blue oblong object. I recognized it immediately.

I reached for the device, but Dixon pulled it away as he stood, then closed the case and put it away. "One other thing." Dixon offered me his hand, which I took. "I'll be in touch."

He saw himself out of the door, and I turned toward Alena. Silence passed between us for several minutes until we were certain no one lurked outside the door.

The Agency said messages with further directions would be delivered to me but never said how. Major Dixon could be the mode of delivery, or he could be something else altogether. Whatever the case, whether I could call Dixon an ally or adversary was now inconsequential. Could I trust him? The oblong object within the box confirmed he had been recruited by the same individuals who called themselves The Agency.

"Is that?" Alena asked.

I handed her the object. As she examined it, Alena opened her mouth to speak just as something on the table caught my attention. I raised my finger to my lips and nodded toward the table and the file Dixon had produced earlier. I picked it up and assessed its weight. Opening it, I pulled out a single page containing a handwritten note. -- Phase Two is beginning.

5

Phase One entailed setting the stage for instability. We had been fortunate to have avoided the loss of human life, but the destruction of Zone Five cost billions of dollars. It also created an atmosphere of fear and uncertainty within the bunker. I hadn't been told how Phase One would play out.

They had approached me one evening well over ten years ago. They knew my work, even though I'd been a government contractor for only a few years. At the time, I'd advanced quickly in my department, overseeing installation projects designed for hundreds of years of stable and sustainable life underground. Bunker Nine was one of many sites I'd visited. By design, it was the most technologically advanced.

When they approached me, I hadn't even considered the possibility of a future coup. Why would I? I was happily married with two young children. I was thinking of creating a future for them. Alena and I had been enjoying an anniversary dinner, and Samantha and Jordan, six and four at the time, at home with a sitter.

While not the fanciest of establishments, the restaurant served several options for three to five-course meals. When Alena and I arrived that night, the Maître d' informed us they had reassigned us to a new table due to scheduling conflicts. They gave us an upgrade on the house. Alena was thrilled at the special treatment, especially when they escorted us to a private booth with a curtain.

I should've known something was up. Like Alena, I didn't put up a fight. Instead, I played it as though I had planned this little charade for her. Sometime into the second course, the curtain pulled back, our meal interrupted by two official though mostly nondescript individuals, one man and one woman. I assumed they were government agents. Like something out of *Men in Black*, they wore matching black suits and black sunglasses. Neither took off their sunglasses. As the man sat, the woman glanced into the dining room and closed the curtains.

Neither my wife nor I had spoken. We were both too shocked, though I did muster the wherewithal to speak. The woman obviously sensed this and held up her hand.

"Mr. and Mrs. Davis. We intend to disrupt this establishment. While essential for our survival, human life is not our primary concern in the immediate, and we will use deadly force. We have to keep the bigger picture in front of us. Control and genetic perfection are primary, and we are conscripting you into our service."

They waited for that to sink in as Alena and I exchanged glances. I stood and laughed.

"Tell me this is some kind of joke."

The man held out his hand, producing nine blue oblong devices that fitted in his palm. "When the time is right, you'll receive instructions on what to do with these."

He pulled my hand toward his and passed off the devices. Once in my hands, I examined them more closely. They were matte blue and weighed a little more than a handful of paper clips. Turning one over, I discovered tiny ridge marks, then held it up.

"Exactly what purpose do these serve?"

"As I said—"

"These," the woman said, "will improve the overall function of the systems within each bunker."

"That's highly unlikely," I said, then stood and turned to Alena. "I do believe it's time for us to go."

The woman stepped into our pathway. "Refusing us will not go well for you or your family."

The man stood. "But trust us when we tell you, you and your family will be safe if you do this one thing for us."

When they took their leave, Alena scrutinized the devices still in my hand. Then she pushed my hand away and took a step back.

"Chet, what have we gotten ourselves into? Control? Genetic purity?"

I folded the devices into a napkin and slid them into the inside pocket of my blazer. "Your guess is as good as mine. We'll find out soon enough, I suppose."

Eight years later, near the completion of Bunker Nine, I received an unmarked envelope in my box at work. I squirreled it away until I got home, and my wife and children were asleep.

I slipped out of the covers and crept out to the garage where I had left the envelope secure in the glove box of my car. Seated, I popped the glove box open. With meticulous care, I slid the paper out of the envelope and unfolded it.

You are the initiator of Phase One. Install each device into the compressor units of the control HVAC system. Further instruction will follow, providing you survive the end of Phase One.

My heart raced as I reread the instructions. I thought of the ridged backs I'd run my fingers over dozens of times in the last few years. Would they really fit seamlessly into the compressor units? If so, they were chips designed for that express purpose, but I had yet to ascertain the function the chips served. The agents had referred to control and genetic purity, but how would these chips enable anyone to accomplish both?

"Why are you up so late?"

I turned to face Alena, who stood with arms crossed several feet away from me.

"A letter with further instruction." I handed the letter to Alena

"The HVAC refers to the bunkers, right? You realize you could potentially sabotage the project and endanger future lives." Her brow furrowed.

I shrugged. "More likely, if I don't go through with this, it'll be our lives instead, and they'll find someone else."

Her face clouded. "What are they even planning?"

Two years passed between the time I completed the installation of the devices and the eruption of Yellowstone. Another year passed underground, and I was promoted to chief engineer of Bunker Nine. In their test phases, the HVAC systems worked better than expected. Though I didn't tell my superiors, I suspected the devices had something to do with it.

Nothing about those devices indicated they would cause an explosion in Zone Five. I had assumed they simply improved the overall effectiveness of the HVAC systems. I couldn't have been more wrong.

Since the mechanical room explosion, we hadn't received word from the other bunkers, which left me to conclude eight similar explosions had occurred. Only some poor S.O.B. in the other bunkers would've likely been called, as I had been, but they would have been incinerated, along with any other victim trapped inside their zones.

Still, even at this stage, the plan had yet to be revealed. More than ever, I was one of several pawns on a chess board, too afraid to ignore an order.

6

We operate in the shadows, often blind to the grand plan. Yet we follow unquestioningly. See this mission through.

The sweat from the palm of my hand soaked into the crumpled note I grasped as I marched toward Ortiz's office. Who was I kidding? I was just a pawn on the chess board, the ark. Still, even a pawn can be transformed into the most powerful piece on the board. I had to believe I could serve a higher purpose even as I floundered in the darkness.

Ortiz had summoned me to his quarters for a reason.

A status update was due, but I resolved to confess my involvement in this plot to the governor. I'd likely face a court-martial, then death if I were lucky.

The steel catwalk beneath my feet betrayed my misgivings as my footsteps clanked unsteadily on my descent to level one of Zone Two, where Governor Ortiz awaited my arrival.

Once on the main floor, someone brushed against my shoulder. I glanced over, and Major Dixon's eyes met mine. I hadn't anticipated an escort.

"Listen—"

"Keep your eyes forward."

I returned my gaze toward Ortiz's quarters.

"Welcome to the new order." Dixon slipped something into my hand. "Discreetly pop this into your mouth before entering."

I stopped. "What is this?"

Dixon's eyes locked onto mine. "The difference between life and death."

He pivoted and continued forward toward Ortiz's quarters. I followed as we closed the distance from two hundred paces to one hundred, then the final fifty. What did I have to lose? I feigned a cough and covered my mouth. The pill landed on my tongue. I nodded to one of two guards at Ortiz's door as the pill dissolved into a bittersweet liquid I swallowed. The guards opened the door, and Major Dixon and I entered.

Priceless paintings decorated the walls of Ortiz's quarters. Like a captain's quarters, it served as an office and residents. Though three times larger than the rest of the residential quarters, I didn't envy the lifestyle but mildly appreciated the artwork. On the walls, I recognized Salvador Dali's *The Sacrament of the Last Supper* and *Crocifisso*. I wondered if the originals hung on the walls or if these were perfect copies. Either way, both seemed simultaneously out of place and suitable for the living quarters of the man who governed a glorified fall-out shelter.

Dressed in a grey pinstripe and a brightly covered tie, Governor Ortiz entered from a door on the far side of the room. "Gentlemen, take a seat."

He gestured toward the Victorian-style furniture, likely transported from what was once the Governor's mansion. Dixon and I sat, and I struggled to find a comfortable position. Ortiz chose to remain standing.

"Status update?" Ortiz asked.

Still uncertain why I had been summoned to this meeting, I glanced at Major Dixon. He nodded, and I spoke first.

"All systems are stable in the remaining four zones. Communication has yet to be re-established with our counterparts in the other eight bunkers." I cleared my throat. "But there is something else."

Dixon stood. "Sir. You're aware there is a faction among us planning a mutiny."

Ortiz shrugged it off while my heart raced. Had I come all this way to be outed by Major Dixon? I barely knew the man, and this shadow organization had yet to reveal itself truly. Ortiz wouldn't have believed me even if I confessed to planting the devices. I shifted forward in my seat. Dixon motioned for me to remain seated as he continued his speech.

"Governor, I am certain you are also aware of the dissatisfaction among the people. Each is closely monitored and what they whisper in the privacy of their homes speaks volumes. We are on the verge of unrest, and the recent lockdowns and mandatory curfews have done nothing to ease their restlessness."

The governor stood there a moment, staring blankly past us. Major Dixon slipped a hand into his pocket and pulled out a small rod, his thumb poised on a button. When Dixon raised the rod, the lone guard in the room moved to tackle him. The room filled with gas. I coughed violently and dropped to the floor, where I breathed clean air. Beside me, Dixon did the same, then I thought of Ortiz and the guard and scrambled toward them.

Dixon pulled me back. "They're already gone."

As the air cleared, I saw the guard and Ortiz. Boils formed on their skin, and their hands clutched frozen at their throats.

"But why?"

"Your wife will explain. Follow me."

Before I could process the first part of Dixon's statement, he darted out the door. I did the same and found myself amid what I could only describe as an organized mob. Around me, the few guards on duty were either unconscious or being wrestled to the ground. A siren blared, and lights flashed, bringing the chaos around me to a screeching halt. A familiar voice conveying poise and presence filled the space.

"Residents of Bunker Nine, your freedom is underway. You are asked to return to your quarters and await further instruction."

Major Dixon turned toward me and grinned. "Just wait to see what we have in store for you."

Two sets of hands grabbed hold of my arms and pinned them behind my back.

"We've got to move," Dixon shouted.

The guards pivoted and shoved me through the mob.

7

Time stood still as I waited in what could only be described as a holding cell. Bare walls echoed my every movement. A steel door barred the way between me and the illusion of freedom beyond this room.

Major Dixon and two armed guards had escorted me to this room hours ago. I had recognized Gary, one of the guards from my rounds. His face, however, conveyed the look of hardened steel, and he barely glanced at me before he and his partner shoved me through the fray of the mob.

When they brought me to the holding cell where I awaited Dixon's promise to come to fruition, I racked my brain. They had placed me under arrest, of that I was sure. Though I didn't pull the proverbial trigger, I also wasn't in a position to cast blame on Major Dixon. I'd take the fall for Ortiz's death. God only knew how The Agency that had coerced me into this mess would react when they discovered I was no longer in play. It didn't matter; no one would believe me if I unveiled my unwitting involvement.

But was I really so innocent? My engineering and HVAC training never once encountered those devices. They weren't necessary for improving the bunker systems, but I certainly didn't protest. I still believed the bunkers held humanity's last hope. The air above would mean sudden death for some and prolonged and painful death for others. Humanity had cancer, emphysema, and C.O.P.D. to look forward to.

Still, I had to get out of this holding cell, then get my family out of this bunker. Correction, I had to get my children out of this bunker. I couldn't trust Alena after hearing her voice so clear and commanding over the P.A. system. Ongoing reading of the above ground still indicated high levels of toxicity. Despite this, I had to believe we could survive the trek to safety. The volcanic ash couldn't have impacted the northernmost parts of Canada and the southernmost parts of Mexico. We could settle down there, my kids and I, and leave my wife to this underground hell. Alena could have it.

She'd betrayed me, but I didn't know the breadth or depth of that betrayal. Had I been a plaything in her hands all this time, moving to her every whim? Or did The Agency or some other faction group recruit her to oppose The Agency? The secrets I kept, I kept from others, but not from her. She had been there from the beginning, and she'd see this, whatever it was, through to the end.

But I'd fight her from every corner; I had to. Fuck control and genetic perfection. Fuck genetic diversity, too. Whoever They were could lie in the shit they'd created. They'd used me to build the perfect fall-out shelters capable of sustaining life for hundreds of years if it came to that. They'd also used me to destroy a good fifth of Bunker Nine and likely the other eight remaining bunkers.

I laughed, and the walls echoed my laughter.

Fuck humanity's survival as well. Humanity had to have survived somewhere beyond the reaches of Yellowstone's Supervolcano. The U.S., despite popular opinion, does not represent the whole of humanity, nor does humanity's hope rest on the survival of the U.S.

I had to find my kids, and we had to get above the ground. I'd planned for this possibility and had four respirators ready to go. The challenge was to get them.

The room echoed to the release of the steel door's bolt. The door opened, and Major Dixon entered. I stood, and my sudden movement sent the chair crashing to the floor.

Major Dixon grinned. "Please, Chet. We're here on a friendly visit. No need for dramatics. But, I think it's time we were clear about a few things."

8

"You better get talking," I shouted at Dixon.

He continued to grin, completely unfazed and directed his attention to the cell door. I followed his gaze until a woman entered.

She wore heels and a dark, finely pressed pants suit with a matching top. I didn't recognize her until she sat down in front of me, right beside Major Dixon.

I took a step forward. "Alena?"

Alena cleared her throat and averted her eyes toward Major Dixon, who nodded. She looked back at me and forced a tight smile.

"Listen, Chet." Alena hesitated. "Please, you should sit for this."

Too stunned to protest, I did as my wife directed

and picked up my chair, and sat across from the pair. She reached her hand across the table in what I took to be an attempt to offer comfort or show a sign of solidarity. I didn't return the gesture.

Major Dixon cleared his throat. "I think it's time, don't you?"

Alena folded her hand into her lap and nodded. "Chet, you won't like what I'm about to tell you, so please—"

"Just get on with it," I said.

"Very well," Alena said. "The eruption. The government was prepared for it. That's why the bunkers were built in the first place. That's also why you were trained to be the best engineer for the project."

I swallowed hard. Alena's mouth moved, and she became ever increasingly animated. Beside her, Major Dixon nodded as they exchanged occasional glances during the explanation as if they were coconspirators letting the victim of a long-running sick joke in on the fun they'd had. Only this wasn't a joke, and no one was having fun.

"Davis," Major Dixon said. "You've got to understand. The forced eruption was decades, maybe more, in the making. The government wanted a reset. Genetic purification and all that."

I slammed my fists onto the table and seethed, directing my rage at Alena. "Tell me. Was our marriage even real?"

Behind them, the doors opened. I rose to my feet as four armed guards swarmed up. Two flanked Dixon and Alena, and the other two restrained me.

Major Dixon rose. "Davis, your marriage isn't

relevant anymore. We're braving a whole new world."

"What about those who are dead?" I shouted and wrestled against the guards who tightened their grips. "Alena! How deep does this thing go?"

Alena and Dixon turned away from me.

"Did you set me up that night at the restaurant?"

Alena froze, then turned and faced me. "Chet, you fool. We were all set up. Can't you see that?"

"What does that even mean?"

Dixon turned to the guards. "Take him to a cell."

He and Alena exited without another glance at me. I shouted expletives at them through the closing doorway, to no avail.

A guard nudged me. "Let's go, Mr. Davis."

I pushed him off. "I can walk by myself."

They led me through a dark but short corridor and into a colorless room, bare except for a cot and a pot.

The door slammed and bolted shut. My only thoughts were of my children: they were all I had in life that was certain, or were they a lie, too?

9

I couldn't gauge the passage of time.

Outside the cell, the bunker's artificial light mimicked the passage of time. One day, our leaders told us, one day we will be above ground, and we'll need to be acclimated to the passage of time. While we hardly had the equivalent, we adapted, and only time would tell if we would truly be ready for daylight again. I didn't have the luxury of daylight's cheap imitation in this cell.

Instead, time passed slowly as I counted the rhythmic flicker of light — a bulb, dimly lit, a reprieve to my restless mind and growing hunger.

I projected my frustration and anger outward when hunger morphed into hunger pangs. Toward the agency that roped me in, toward Alena, who had untold secrets of her own, and toward the government for forcing the eruption of the supervolcano. But, most of all, toward myself for allowing myself to be duped.

What had I hoped to gain? The salvation of my family? Saved for what? A lifetime of hard living below ground? Or perhaps struggling against scorched earth and ash while fending off savages taking advantage of the lawless state that would become the U.S.?

I scoffed, and my voice echoed mockingly. I realized I no longer hungered. I had endured the pangs of starvation, and I had endured the solitude. Death beckoned me, and I would soon be its guest.

Nonetheless, mental clarity rushed over me. My kids needed me, and I had a plan for getting us out of here.

The cell door creaked open, and I shielded my eyes from the light that flooded into the room. Two silhouettes approached.

A voice like gravel chuckled. "Looks like he has risen."

The other squatted and effortlessly pulled me to my feed. "Can you stand?"

"Yes," I croaked.

One of them handed me a canteen and a few crackers. "After all that time," he said. "You'll need to take small sips."

I did as I was told, then wiped my mouth. "How long?"

"A few days," one said, and the other contradicted him with, "A few weeks."

"We haven't been here long," the second guard said.

The other ground out another response. "Follow us."

They turned and walked away without so much as waiting for a question. I had about one hundred of them.

We followed a familiar maze of catwalks and tunnels integrated throughout the entire bunker. I didn't require an escort as they took me to Zone Five, where the once-sealed doors stood open.

Beyond these doors, hundreds of uniformed men and women loaded gear onto armored vehicles or busied themselves in some fashion as they carried stamped boxes from one end of the zone to another.

One of the guards gave me a gentle shove, and I didn't need further prompting. Not until they led me to a makeshift office space where a woman typed vigorously on the computer. I noted the single camera mounted in the corner of the room. The woman turned and smiled at me. Alena.

10

She motioned for me to sit down and folded her hands in front of her on the desk. As she spoke, she maintained the same forced smile.

"Chet, I trust you're being treated well."

I shrugged. "Considering my wife had me locked up

in a goddamn cell."

She dismissed the guards and leaned closer to me when the door closed. "I don't like this any more than you do, so if you cooperate, we can move past all this."

I choked back the urge to slap her, then took a deep breath. "To what end?"

She picked up a remote and dimmed the lights. I didn't trust her, but I had to go along with her plans for now. A projector screen lowered from the ceiling to our right, where an image of a metropolis appeared.

"You're looking at what remains of the U.S. Government. It must be eliminated if we are to survive."

"I assume the 'we' are those who possess the genetic diversity for repopulation."

She nodded. "And our family."

I doubted that included me, but I had to know what she had planned. "I'm one man."

"You're the perfect trigger man," Alena corrected me.

I scoffed. "Or the perfect chump."

She ignored my comment and clicked the remote. An armory appeared on the screen. "Our sources tell us the last of our nation's leadership is hunkered below ground."

"And you want me to do what exactly?"

She handed me a dossier. "It's time for a hard reset."

The plan was simple. Head northeast, get inside as an HVAC man and plant a few explosives. Then skedaddle before the whole thing blows. It was a shit plan that didn't guarantee my survival. Not that I expected it to. Anarchy rarely comes with guarantees. Still, going along with the plan would buy me some time.

"I leave at 0200."

She nodded. "I assume you accept."

What the hell? I nodded my consent.

"Good," Alena said as she stood.

I did the same as she walked around the desk. She flung her arms around me and planted her lips on mine. She smelled of lilacs, and my lips gave way to hers. As suddenly as she initiated our exchange, she pulled away. Her eyes, filled with passion and pleading, met mine.

She had maneuvered us, so I stood between her and the camera's line of sight. She mouthed the words, Get the children, before she came onto me once more. This time, I returned her passionate kisses.

11

Four hours until departure didn't leave me much time. I passed through corridors and crossed over catwalks as I headed toward our family's apartment. Though I didn't know the full extent of Alena's involvement with The Agency or her apparent double-cross, I had to trust she had our children's best interests in mind. Maybe she'd gone in too deep, or maybe her display of passion was just an act.

I flipped through the dossier again. At best, I would shake up what was left of the U.S. government and send them swarming throughout the countryside, uprooting The Agency dead set on toppling them. I could make it through the front doors of the armory and find my way into the central hub of the HVAC systems. The Agency, or Alena, chose me precisely because I had the credentials and clearances. I could do it, but my involvement would gain nothing and cost me everything. Saving my children and getting the hell out of this bunker was a better option. And 0200 fast approached.

"Kids," I called out as I barged through the apartment door. "Sam? Jordan?"

"Here," Jordan hissed.

He and Sam sat on the couch. Beside Sam sat her boyfriend, Nick. The three of them held small bags in their laps.

"Mom said it's okay if he comes," Sam said, nudging herself closer to Nick.

I thought of the access panel in Zone One and the items I had stashed away.

"Fine," I said. "Mom'll have to catch up with us later."

The kids nodded, and we waited until darkness set over the bunker and the last chime of the night rang out, signaling curfew.

I nodded to the kids, and they followed me to the back of the apartment, where we surrounded a small utility closet. A stack of seven boxes made very little room for general maintenance work. But that mattered very little. Access to the panel behind the boxes would open up to a maze of interconnecting ductwork and tunnels, all of which would lead us to Zone One and our freedom.

Jordan, Sam, and Nick assisted in the relocation of

the boxes while I loosened the panel and placed it to the side of the opening. I turned to the kids.

"Climb up and move to the right and wait for me. Once I'm up, you'll follow me."

They nodded and climbed through the opening. As I stuck my head through the opening, a pounding came at the front door. I cursed under my breath. Either the night watchman had spotted the lights on in the hallway, or someone waited outside to see me off to complete my mission to topple the skeletal remains of the U. S. Government.

I switched off the light and waited. Silence ticked off the moments, and I stepped inside the utility closet and closed the door behind me. I crawled through the opening and did my best to slide the panel back in place. I didn't test its security. I only hoped it held long enough for us to make our escape.

I climbed up, hung a left, and behind me, the kids eased their way over the opening below and followed. We had only to endure the heat and tedious nature of pausing to keep from alerting the patrol below to our movement above.

Hours passed without commotion from the residents and guards below. I checked the time: 0030. The dossier indicated 0200 for reporting to the main gate. That gave us an hour's head start if we didn't hit any snags in the next half hour. I only hoped the ash had settled enough at this point to keep us from leaving footprints to mark our escape.

12

Below me, a guard paced back and forth on the outermost point of Zone One. For what purpose? Only I knew of the stash of supplies I'd hidden behind the access door just out of our reach. It was possible Alena had tracked my movements all this time, but to what end? Especially with the safety of our children on the line.

Behind me, one of the kids shifted their weight and sent sound ricocheting off the walls. We froze as the guard looked up and waited.

Mercifully, the clanging from above began again. Below us, the guard cursed and moved on. I shimmied forward until I reached a cornered-off section where a vent opened to a chamber, wherein lay my supplies, untouched and tucked away. I looked over my shoulder. Three sets of eyes filled with expectation met mine. I nodded, popped the vent open, and crawled out. Crouching, I helped out Jordan, Sam, and Nick, and led them on hands and knees toward our supplies.

I pulled out four packages of masks and handed them out. I did the same with goggles and explained, "Wear these at all times. Or until we can be sure the air is safe."

They nodded and donned masks and goggles. I slipped a bag over my shoulder and indicated the kids should do the same. From proper protection to packaged food and access to clean water, these bags would be sufficient until we made it outside the radius of soot and ash that likely covered the desert above.

Motioning for the kids to follow as I shuffled to the access door above, I cranked the hand wheel to the left and one lock released. I continued to turn the wheel until I heard three more clicks and a gentle hiss. The door popped open, and I shielded my eyes from the light above. The kids did the same.

Somehow, we'd lost track of time below ground. I climbed out, quickly aware of my mistake. Flood lights mounted on the top of two military-style Humvees marked our location. A figure, silhouetted by the lights, approached.

"Mr. Davis?" the figure asked.

I raised my right hand in a wave.

"Let me guess?" I asked. "Phase Three?"

Behind me, Sam spoke. "Dad, what's going on?"

"Fuck me," the figure said. "You brought your kids?"

I nodded, and the figure sighed.

"Come along," the figure said. He turned and walked toward the Humvee. We followed.

13

As daylight broke through the cloud of ash still layering the air around us, I glimpsed remnants of a once proud country we'd never see again. A toppled monument here and a crumbling state house there. Even outside the uninhabitable epicenter of Yellowstone's eruption, much of the country remained desolate.

From the side of the road, a grimy child stood by his mother, who rooted through a pile of rubble. When we passed, he waved at us. I waved back. In the backseat, Jordan, Sam, and Nick wore expressions of empathetic suffering. This would be their inheritance. Not the glossy malls or the clean parks where families drove their vans for a picnic. No, they would inherit ash and rubble if they remained in this country.

North into Canada was where we should go, where evergreen trees still thrived, though the climate was likely ten to twenty degrees cooler than it should be. Or perhaps we ought to go south into Mexico. Even so, we'd have to pass through the epicenter of the eruption again. But would the Mexican borders be open to citizens of an America that ceased, long before the eruption, to offer hope and refuge to the tired, poor, and huddled masses yearning to breathe freely?

Only time would tell. Until then, I had a job to do. I understood that now. I turned to our driver, the figure who greeted us weeks ago. "How much longer?"

"Another day's drive," he said, glancing at me. "But you're not doing this alone."

Ahead of us, another caravan of Humvees pulled onto the otherwise barren interstate highway.

Our driver turned to me and grinned. "That should be your counterpart from Bunker Seven."

I nodded.

More would come, of that I was certain. We would raze the final remains of an America built upon the tyranny of the fat cats and politicians of D.C. and Wall Street. From the ash and rubble, we would rebuild and live free.

Stanley, Idaho

Travis Millworth

By Jake Cavanah

Chapter 1

Hot air smacked Travis in the face and burned his eyes the second he opened the front door. A suffocating stench blew in the house, bringing with it a discolored cloud of smoke. He looked down at his feet and saw ashy, black rocks. Some were the size of pebbles, but some were bigger than a baseball. Travis was thankful none hit a window.

"Close that damn door, Travis," Tammy said.

Closing the door did nothing to take away either the smell or the burning sensation in his eyes. Travis rested his hands on his knees and squeezed his eyes shut, hoping it would help the pain. He tried breathing through his mouth, but all that did was make him taste and inhale the smoke. He retched, about to throw up, but all that came out were heavy dry heaves that sounded as if he was a dying smoker.

His cough under control, Travis dried his eyes and looked out of the window closest to the front door. Any other day he'd be able to see Sheep Mountain. Now he couldn't even see the lawn chairs only a couple of feet from the window on the porch.

"Goddammit, they're here," James said.

James got off the couch and grabbed a rifle out of the lift-up coffee table. Miller Lite cans slid off the table. Most were empty, but a few spilled on the rug and carpet. James almost slipped on his way to the window where Travis stood. He had his finger on the trigger and aimed his rifle—ready for whoever he thought was coming. The stale beer on James momentarily distracted Travis from the smoke's stink.

"You put that rifle down, James. Ain't no one coming out of there," Calvin said.

James turned around and glared at his brother, oblivious to where the rifle was pointing.

"They're here, Cal. I told you they were comin', and now they here," James said.

"Nothin' out there but that smoke and ash, James. Damn impossible to breathe," Travis said.

"They can do things we can't, boy. They're prepared for this, and we ain't." James turned on Terryn. "Goddammit, shut that baby up!"

James, Calvin, and Tammy glared at Terryn as she

carried her wailing baby back to her and Travis' room. No one spoke until she slammed the door shut.

"I told you they was eventually comin', and now, they're here," James said.

"Let's go check, then," Travis said.

James glanced at Calvin before turning his gaze to the floor, but Travis pressed on, "Well, come on, then. If they out there, we ain't gonna fight 'em off by staying in here."

"Ain't none of us going out there and firing at nothin' we can't see. Let's sit tight before we know what's really going on. Y'all hear?" Calvin said.

Neither James nor Travis said a thing. Calvin cursed under his breath and stormed toward Travis. Calvin grabbed his son by the shirt and pushed him against the front door. He put his nose against Travis' and asked, "You hear me, boy?"

"Yes, Pa, I hear you."

"Look at me when I talk to you, boy!"

The stale beer on Calvin's breath made clear he'd had a good amount to drink. It made Travis' nose wrinkle, and for a second, Travis thought he would throw up. Calvin scrunched Travis' shirt tighter, his other hand on his belt buckle.

Travis forced himself to look his father in the eye and say, "Yes, Pa, I hear you."

Calvin shoved him aside and headed to the kitchen for another beer. Travis caught him give James a dirty look on his way.

"I'm telling ya, Cal, they're out there," James said.

"None of y'all know what's going on out there, so quit acting like you do," Tammy said.

Travis' mother traded the rag she was using to cover up her face for a cigarette. She sucked it down quickly and wasted no time lighting another. Tammy sat at the kitchen table sipping soda from her canteen between puffs—more on edge than usual.

James and Calvin drank their beers, and Tammy smoked in silence while Travis massaged where his father had grabbed him and stared out of the window, searching for *anything* that would tell him what was happening. But there was only silence, smoke, and ash. The air looked so thick, Travis doubted anyone could survive out there without the proper gear. It was so grim he couldn't rule out his uncle's hasty theory, but Travis' gut told him something bigger than people was responsible.

A belch from James broke Travis' focus. He turned toward his family and studied their expressions. Aside from looking drunk, James was trying to hide that he was scared shitless. Not even the soda and cigarettes could take away his mother's anxiety. His father appeared torn between his older brother's theory and logic. They were far from impressive, but they were who would get through whatever this was with him.

Terryn came back to the kitchen to fix her son a bottle. Tammy rolled her eyes when a soft cry came from their bedroom. James tossed his arms in the air and Calvin cursed under his breath. Terryn ran back to their room.

"See if you can get the news on, Cal," Tammy said.

They couldn't get the television on. Calvin and Travis flipped the light switches in the living room and kitchen, but nothing happened; the power out. Travis began putting wood in the fireplace.

"Boy, with all this smoke, you're goin' to light a damn fire?" James asked.

"How else we supposed to see?" Travis asked.

"It's all we got right now, James. Unless you want to go get the generator out the shed," Calvin said.

James grabbed another Miller Lite instead and said, "Open up that chimney and all that ash is gonna get in."

Calvin and Travis exchanged expressions, each acknowledging his point.

"Then, let's go get the generator. We need it, and there's food in the shed. Everything in the fridge is gonna go bad if the power don't come back on. Dammit, Tammy, there's enough damn smoke in here. Put that out," Calvin said.

Tammy crushed her third consecutive cigarette in the ashtray on the kitchen table and glared at Calvin. She took a gulp of soda and tapped her fingers against the table.

"Boy, get the gas masks," Calvin said.

"I'll check the closet," Travis said.

He opened the door and a rifle fell out, harmlessly hitting the ground. Travis set the rifle aside and dug through the mess for the gas masks. Behind rain boots, fleeces, jackets, gloves, knife sets, and ammunition, he found them.

Travis set them at his father's feet, who then said, "Ain't ever had to use 'em before."

Calvin put one on and fit it to him. He tossed Travis a pair and told him to do the same.

"All right. Travis and I are gonna go out there. Get the food and generator. Can you shoot?" Calvin asked

James.

"Guess we'll find out."

Travis saw the irritation in his father's eyes.

"Check on them animals and my garden out there, too, yeah?" Tammy said.

"Not sure if there will be anything to check on, Ma."

Travis grabbed two rifles from the open coffee table for his father and himself and a pistol for his mother. He set it on the table and gave her a look that said, "Watch out for you-know-who" before heading out in the smoke and ash.

The farthest Calvin and Travis could see was to the tip of their rifles. They both aimed as if ready to fire, but given the poor visibility, hitting anything out there was unlikely. The knee-high rock made gaining their footing nearly impossible, throwing them off balance with every step. Not even their utility pants kept the rock from scraping their legs. Some wrong steps hurt more than others and often ripped a hole in their pants or in their work boots. Paying attention to where they were walking while staying ready to shoot required all their focus. The rifle was probably useless, but offered comfort, especially as seeing was getting more difficult.

They couldn't wipe the ash off their masks quickly enough. It stained their skin, making them a chalky gray and black, as if they'd spent all day in a coal mine. Travis wiped his mask to see his hand in front of his face and the ash in the crevices between his fingernails and skin. Ash had buried into his fingers to the extent it lined his fingerprint.

The masks helped but couldn't stave off such a heavy, suffocating stench. Travis' lungs worked harder for less air, and he had no choice but to ignore the pain. Only he and his father could get the supplies back to his family.

The longer they were out there, the more pointless it was to check on the animals and garden.

Calvin and Travis could've walked to the shed, animal pen, and garden blindfolded on any other day, but the smoke, ash, and fear disoriented them, rendering them out of place in their own home. The lack of visibility made the broken car parts, tools, Miller Lite cans, fishing poles, half-deflated rafts, shovels, rakes, tire rims, and other miscellaneous junk more of an obstacle course than before the smoke and ash. Travis almost tripped over one of the rafts when he heard a clunk followed by his father's cursing.

"You all right, Pa?"

"Goddammit. This is why I told y'all to clean this up."

"You all right?"

"Yes, goddammit."

Neither had realized how far they'd wandered from each other until they spoke. Travis trod carefully towards where he heard his father and warned Calvin he was coming to avoid a fatal mistake. Once he was a couple of feet from him, Travis saw his father had cut his leg open badly.

"Can you walk all right?"

Calvin murmured a few curse words before saying he was fine and to shut up.

The shed's structure hadn't been touched in at least

a decade. Time and neglect had transformed the shed into an abandoned wreck. Its condition made Travis feel foolish for depending on it to protect their survival tools. Travis couldn't remember what it looked like without the white paint peeling off. Now he didn't know if he'd ever remember it without this blanket of ash and rock surrounding it.

So much ash sat atop the shed's roof, Travis and his father worried it might collapse, but happy and surprised to find their supplies still intact. An abundance of canned food, dried fruit, water, freeze-dried meat, jerky, lined the shelves; guns, ammo, clips, magazines, extra scopes, knives, blankets, scarves, more gas masks, sleeping bags, axes, lanterns, chopped wood, chainsaws, animal feed, soil, gardening tools, horse halters filled the space in stacks. And the generator. Collectively, the provisions looked more than ample, but neither Travis nor Calvin had any idea if they were enough.

Most of their supplies were thanks to Calvin's and James' father. He bought the property a few decades ago to have a place to prepare for the end of civilization. Stockpiling resources had consumed him. From sunup until it was time to drink, he would build up his supplies and work the land. No one was brave enough to tell him he wasn't all there, but were he alive today, he'd have the last word.

"Don't just stand there, boy. Start putting what we need in that wagon," Calvin said, tending to his leg.

The inside of the shed was dark, but there was no ash or smoke. Travis took off his gas mask and almost rubbed his eyes until he remembered how contaminated his hands were. He squeezed his eyes shut and opened them wide to adjust to the new lighting, or lack thereof. Travis wished he could roll the generator back to the house and load up the wagon with more supplies, but they couldn't risk the layer of ash on the ground damaging their only power source. Getting the wagon through it would be hard enough.

Travis filled up the rest of the wagon with food and water. As soon as the wagon was almost too heavy for him to pull, he laid a blanket over the supplies. Taking back enough for five people and a baby filled the wagon fast. Just by looking at it, Travis knew he'd be back for more sooner rather than later. He scanned the shed one last time before his father and he headed back to the house. All he could do was hope to get through whatever *this* was.

Chapter 2

Travis snuck some food and water back to his and Terryn's room. He had no trouble sneaking it past his parents. Calvin and James were too drunk to notice, and his mother was too busy telling them how clueless, dumb, and drunk they both were. Travis and Terryn heard them becoming more animated from their room. This behavior was nothing new—Travis and Terryn were so accustomed to it, they could predict when the argument would escalate and when it wouldn't.

Terryn rocked Luke back and forth and hummed to him, hoping he'd stay asleep. Travis moved things around in their closet as quietly as possible to make room for their personal stockpile. Once Terryn was sure

Luke was sound asleep, she laid him in his crib.

"What were they talking about when you were out there, Trav?" she asked.

"Besides arguing about their drinking, James was telling Ma and Pa about how we should've been better prepared for this and how *they* are finally here."

Terryn rolled her eyes. She said, "He doesn't know what the hell he's saying half the time."

Travis agreed. "Don't matter, though. If he says it enough and we don't hear nothing else, they gonna start believing him."

"Does Ma?"

"Not now, at least."

"Who are *they*?"

Reluctant to recount the conversation, Travis did anyway. "James thinks the government's finally come for us. He says they're trying to kill everyone who ain't rich by making it impossible to live off the land and work. Him and Pa started arguing because he said Pa didn't prep enough. James said if the property was his, we'd have nothing to worry about."

"James is an idiot. He doesn't know what the hell he's talking about. He's such a drunk."

Travis put his index finger to his mouth and said, "Careful, Terryn."

"Sorry. But you know it's true. There's a reason their daddy left this place to Pa and not him. He'd be even broker and drunker on the streets if it weren't for Pa."

Travis agreed but didn't want to risk saying so. "Dammit, Terryn, you asked me what they said, and I'm telling you."

"I know. I'm sorry. What did Pa say to him?"

"He tried to get him to calm down and stop talking crazy. Pa tried to call John Patterson from down the road but couldn't get through. Then James tried to call a friend from one of their groups. When they didn't answer is when he got real worked up, talking about how they made sure to cut off their phones.

"I don't know what we're gonna do. James and Ma don't work. All the animals are dead, and we're not gonna get anything more from Ma's garden. Doubt there's work out there for Pa. Even if there was, he'd have no way of knowing about it."

"All of the animals are dead?"

Travis nodded and said, "Pa checked on 'em on the way back from the shed, and I checked on Ma's garden. He also said he wanted to head over to John Patterson himself, but I think Ma talked him out of it. The only thing they agreed on was if he's going anywhere, we're going with him."

"It ain't even a mile down the road."

"Go out there yourself and see how long a mile feels."

Terryn inhaled deeply through her nose. "What do you think, Trav?"

Travis rubbed his temples and squeezed his eyes shut. He hadn't had a chance to think for himself since *this* all started. The world became so dark and smoky so quickly. For as insane as James was, no one else had another idea.

"Trav."

"I don't know. It's so damn smoky and ashy out there, I'd swear the world's ending. We're gonna have to make do with what we have here until it clears up. Can't no baby handle all that smoke and ash right now, Terryn. We have to stay put."

"No, Trav. Now is the perfect time. No one would expect it. They won't even be able to see us. This is a blessing, Trav. We can go once they go to sleep tonight. We have enough supplies to get us through a couple weeks. We can take one of the trucks and go. Come on, Trav, we can do—"

"Terryn."

His older sister's desperation smoldered in her expression. Her eyes watered and lips trembled with both fear and excitement—and the uncertainty of what was out there and the possibility their plan was finally coming together.

"Why not, Trav? Why?" she asked just above a whisper.

"Luke would die out there, Terryn. You smelled how bad it was when I barely opened the door. Imagine him out there breathing in all that ash and smoke. He wouldn't make it through the night. Come on.

"Besides, we don't have enough supplies. If we're lucky, all of the supplies on this damn property will last a couple weeks, and what if where we want to go is in worse shape than here? We're stuck right now, Terryn. We're stuck until we figure out what's going on and it clears up out there. All right?"

Travis came off harsher than he meant to. He hated talking to his sister like this, but there were times she was too stubborn for her own good. He had to get his point across.

She covered her mouth and sobbed. Tears and drool

drenched her hands, and her body buckled over. Travis and she had been talking about starting over somewhere else for so long. They had finally built up enough courage to do it. Now it was just a matter of timing.

"I can't do a damn thing right, Trav. I can't give Luke a daddy, and I can't get out of this goddamn house. I fuckin' hate it here!"

Travis didn't have to put his finger over his mouth for Terryn to know she was being too loud. She wasn't fast enough to regain her composure.

"The hell are you yelling and crying for?" Calvin asked from the doorway. A rifle hung over his shoulder and a pistol on his belt. What the beer did to his eyes made him more intimidating.

"Nothing, Pa, nothing," Terryn said. She wiped her hands dry on her shirt.

"You're gonna wake up that damn baby," he said.

Their father turned his attention towards Travis and said, "Need you in the kitchen."

"Yes, Pa."

"Give this to your sister, too" Calvin said. He handed Travis a lantern. "Careful how much you use it," Calvin said. His tone implied this would be his last helpful gesture.

Travis didn't have to look at their father to know he was scowling at Terryn. He promised himself he'd get his sister out as soon as possible. He just had to figure out how.

James smacked the side of the television in the belief that would turn it on. He yelled about what a piece of shit it was and complained about not having any wrestling to watch. Tammy sat on the couch and stared aimlessly ahead. A full ashtray and soda canteen were on the coffee table in front of her. Travis found the house smokier now than when he opened the door.

"Goddammit, James, it ain't gonna turn on. Give it a rest," Calvin said.

James bit his upper lip and glared at Calvin. He was so out of breath, his chest heaving up and down. His eyes were redder and glassier than Calvin's, and he looked more swollen than usual. But he listened to his younger brother and sat next to Tammy.

"They're takin' all we've got from us, dammit. They're takin' it all!" James said.

Calvin ignored James and said, "Sit down, boy."

Travis sat on the opposite side of his mother. More guns were on the coffee table than were there earlier. Calvin caught him eyeing them and said, "We need to defend this property."

Travis nodded and waited for further instructions.

"Whatever's going on could keep us here a long time. We need to be careful with how much we use every day. Some days, some of us maybe ain't gonna be able to eat, but those are sacrifices we'll have to make," Calvin said.

"What're—" Travis uttered.

"You, me, and James are gonna take turns watching the house every night. Got enough guns here to fight anyone off. Imagine even the worst folks in town won't try anything too crazy in these conditions, but we can't rule shit out. Best to be too careful than not careful enough."

James snarled and said, "Goddammit, we need more

men, Cal. They're going to come and it's just gonna be us three shootin' into the smoke hoping we hit one. Daddy told us one day they'd be comin' for us, but we've just been on our asses thinkin' we'll be able to stop 'em alone. Look what they already done!"

"Ain't no one ever stopped you from doing something, James. Said you could've gotten your own men and set 'em up in one of the empty sheds, but you were just too damn lazy to do it. So why don't you just keep your mouth shut? You ain't ever been any help.

"You can help now by getting ready for when it's your turn to watch because that's when we'll actually need your two cents. You understand?"

Travis and his mother exchanged brief expressions of surprise at how Calvin spoke to his brother. Typically, James talked down to Calvin, but there was a shift in their dynamic. And all four of them felt it.

"How are two men and a boy gonna defend the property, Cal? They're gonna come for us and take every last bit of what we have, and ain't none of us gonna be able to do nothin' about it."

"Won't just be you fighting 'em off," Tammy said.

James looked to the ceiling and scoffed.

"What, you don't think I can shoot?" Tammy asked.

James was obviously about to make a snarky comment until he noticed Calvin's glare.

"Can shoot better than a drunk," Tammy said under her breath.

"Who's watching tonight?" Travis asked, thankful to break the tension.

"You. James and me are gonna makc sure all these guns are ready to shoot, and she's gonna start portioning out the food so we know how much we can eat every day," Calvin said.

"Okay. What about Terryn?" Travis asked.

"What about her?" Calvin said.

"What can she do to help?" Travis asked.

"That girl ain't ever done anything around here except cause trouble. Don't think she's gonna start now," Tammy said.

"Let Terryn worry about that baby. That's more than enough responsibility for her," Calvin said.

"Could have two women helpin' us stay fed, but instead we only got one because the other is too busy carin' for a baby with no daddy. I swear if she was mine, I'd kick her a—"

"Shut up, James. The sooner you quit complaining, the better off we'll be," Calvin said.

Travis considered punching James in the face and probably would've if it weren't for the man outside.

"Cal! Cal!"

Calvin and Travis each picked up a rifle and ran to the door. James sat looking helplessly at Tammy.

"Who's out there?" Calvin said.

"It's John. Come to make sure y'all are doing okay."

"It's John," Calvin said.

"Let him in, Cal," James said.

"What? We're just letting everyone in now," Calvin said.

"He ain't just anyone," James said.

James and Calvin stared hard at each other.

"You alone, John?" Calvin asked.

Travis heard Luke crying and Terryn shuffling

around. Calvin sighed and James rolled his eyes. Tammy lit up another cigarette.

"Yeah, I'm alone," John said.

"Come on in then," Calvin said.

John Patterson had been the Millworths' neighbor for as long as Travis could remember. He was older than Calvin but not old enough to be Travis' grandfather. Travis hadn't ever seen John without a big lip of tobacco, and tonight was no different. He wore his typical overalls over a way-too-slim-fitting white t-shirt. It had yellow sweat stains under his arms, and the neck was scrunched up. The only reason Travis knew it was originally white was because it was the only shirt he ever wore. Now it was gray because of the ash. Travis wasn't sure if what he was smelling was smoke that followed John in or John himself.

"Y'all been out there yet?" John asked.

"My boy and I went out there to get some supplies," Calvin said.

"Hope you got more than that, Cal," John said.

"There's more in the shed," Calvin said.

John nodded, but it was obvious he had his doubts.

"What the hell you think *this* is, John?" James asked.

John let out a deep breath and crossed his arms. "Reckon they're finally comin' for us. Ruinin' our land and takin' away the little we have is the first way they'll hit us. I'd think this is only the beginning. That's why we gotta do everythin' we can to fight 'em off. Gotta stick together."

"How'd you get over here?" Calvin asked.

"Walked. Took me damn near forty-five minutes. All that smoke and ash made that trip a lot longer than it's ever been."

"You gonna be okay?" Calvin asked.

John nodded. He said, "Some dead crops and animals are gonna hurt, but I've only got myself to worry about. I'll be okay. It's what we do this for, right?"

"Got that right. It'll be dark before you know it with all that smoke in the air. Welcome to stay here if you want, John," James said.

"I appreciate that. Sure I won't be too much of a burden?"

"Not for one night," Calvin said.

John nodded. "Thanks. I'll be sure to make up for what I use tomorrow. Wouldn't want your family short on supplies because of old John Patterson now."

"Tammy, get John a beer now," Calvin said.

Tammy grabbed three beers. After they took their first sip, Calvin said, "Your watch starts soon, boy."

Travis left them to their beers and prepared for the night.

Chapter 3

Night 1 Journal

Pa, James, and John must've been up past midnight. I don't know how much beer we have, but if they drink like that every night, we'll probably be out soon. James and John were talking their heads off about what they think is happening. They were saying stuff like how they knew this would happen a long time ago. James kept saying how he wished his daddy was here to fight them off. He thinks he's the only one in town who knows a damn thing about anything, but everyone knows he's a drunk. If it weren't for Pa, James would probably be dead. His fat ass is snoring on the couch right now. I wish he'd just die in his sleep. There'd be more supplies for us, and then we wouldn't have to listen to him anymore.

I'm not sure why Pa let John stay here. He's a good neighbor and nice, but Pa knows we don't have enough supplies to take care of someone else. Maybe John isn't as prepared as he says. Something about him being here is off, and I think there'll be trouble.

It's times like this when I feel the worst for Terryn. Pa lets a neighbor stay here during this but says taking care of Terryn and Luke is a pain. Luke's just a baby. He doesn't need much food. He definitely cries a lot and he's loud, but he doesn't take up that much space. Grandparents are supposed to love their children and grandchildren, no matter what. Maybe Pa and Ma don't love Luke because he doesn't have a daddy, but that's not Luke's fault.

I'm supposed to watch out for attackers, but I'm starting to think there aren't any. Even if there was a full moon, it would be impossible to see anything. My lantern's barely helping me see this. I took my mask off, but it only took a few seconds to feel like I was going to cough up a lung. It's still really smoky out here, but I can't really see it. Everything just looks darker than it normally would. I know ash is still falling because it keeps getting on my mask. I have to wipe it every five minutes so I can at least see a little bit.

Whatever happened yesterday happened so fast. Dark clouds of smoke came out of nowhere and made the sun go away. We were all really scared, but no one looked more scared than James did. I hope Pa doesn't let him off the hook if we have to fight because I know he won't make it. He can barely shoot something that's not moving.

Sitting out here isn't as scary as I thought it'd be. I still am sort of scared, but if I can't see anything, then no one else can. James told Pa and John that the people attacking us have stuff that makes them see in the smoke. That way, they can shoot us, but we can't shoot them. John and Pa I think believed him, but I don't because James says crazy stuff like that a lot.

I don't know what I believe, though. Nothing like this has ever happened, but it reminds me of when we had those really bad fires a couple years ago. I remember how everything in the sky was orange. The sun turned really red but when that happened, we had more time to get the animals inside, so none of them died. Some of the crops died, but Ma kept most of them alive. A little ash ended up on the trucks and roof, but it was nothing like it is now. If this was because of another fire, this one is a lot bigger.

I want to see how much time I have left, but Pa said I can't go inside until he comes out and gets me in the morning. I'm hoping I don't have much longer because I'm hungry and thirsty, and my lantern might not make it much longer. The sky isn't getting any brighter, but I hope that's just because the smoke and ash are blocking it. The only thing I can do right now is wait for Pa to come get me. Until then, I'll be watching out for whatever this is.

Chapter 4

"What good are you gonna be if you're asleep?"

Calvin kicked Travis hard enough that he knocked the wind out of him. The prospect of choking on his vomit scared Travis enough to hold it.

"Get up. Breakfast is ready, and we have work to do," Calvin said.

Travis groaned and rolled around on the patio before getting up. He caught his father laughing and shaking his head. He looked down: ash covered him from head to toe. Travis did his best to shake it off but most had already penetrated his clothes.

James and John sniggered when he walked inside for the same reason. Tammy rolled her eyes, but Travis wasn't sure if it was at him, or his uncle and John.

"Sit. I'll fetch you some breakfast," Tammy said.

"Thanks, Ma."

"I'd ask you how it was out there, but it seems like the night had its way with you. That's what happens when you fall asleep on the job," James said. He laughed and sipped his beer.

"At least someone was out there. Not everyone can just sit in here getting drunk," Travis said.

That statement earned Travis a smack to the back of his head.

"Careful how you come in talking. Might cost you breakfast," Tammy said.

Travis looked at his mother apologetically, but not

his uncle.

"The hell you think you are talkin' to me like that boy? Gonna have to teach you something your parents didn't. I'll show you how my daddy would've done it," James said.

James stood up and kicked his chair backward. He almost had his belt out of his pant loops before Calvin stepped in.

"You best put that away, James. Anyone here takes a belt to my boy, it's me. You got that? Sit back down and eat your damn breakfast," Calvin said.

James obeyed his younger brother. Calvin wasn't in the mood to hear it, but James didn't care.

"You know, if our daddy heard him talk to me like that, know what he would've done? He would've taken his belt and hit him so hard your boy's face would've been swollen for a month. Boy, he'd be in so much pain he'd be crying louder than that damn baby over there. Tell you what, Cal, he's lucky to have a daddy like you 'round to protect him."

"And you're lucky my daddy gave you a place to live," Travis said under his breath.

"Boy, you have somethin' else to say?"

"Enough, goddammit. Shut up before I lock both of you outside. Goddammit," Calvin said.

Calvin's scolding silenced Travis and James but woke up Luke.

"Oh, goddammit," Calvin said.

"Man, you Millworths are a good time. I wouldn't want to be with anyone else right now," John said.

Travis nearly forgot about their house guest. John, too, had a breakfast beer and was scarfing down food he hadn't worked for. Travis watched him enjoy the few resources his family had with contempt. A tense silence fell over the breakfast table. Terryn was trying to get Luke to stop crying in their room. Travis was thankful she didn't have too much trouble doing so. His family was more on edge than usual, which was when their behavior became the most unpredictable.

The silence continued after Luke quieted down. The only sounds at the table were chewing, utensils scraping against plates, and James burping after every sip of beer until John gave his two cents.

"I tried gettin' through to some folks closer to town but couldn't talk long because the channel went fuzzy. I did hear though that the power's still out. Only thing that works is generators, so, we're lucky this one's good. I think it's best if we stay here 'til we know what's goin' on. Maybe the smoke will clear and we'll be able to see better. Shootin' out in these conditions, we won't hit a thing, but you can bet whoever's after us sure can."

"Damn right they can. They've been waitin' years to come after us like this. We need to make every shot count. We're happy you came, John," James said.

"Happy to help. Just got to stay alert and keep these sons of bitches away from what's ours," John said.

James nodded in agreement. They clinked beer cans and took a drink.

"Any way you can go back home and bring over some supplies?" Calvin asked.

John looked at him like he was crazy. "Not in these conditions, Cal. Too hard to get from point A to point B when it's like this, but after we can see better and know what's goin' on, I'd be happy to."

Calvin hardened his stare. "But you came over when it was like this, John. You're under my roof, and you don't expect to contribute?"

"He's a good shot, Cal. Better than him," James said, nodding at Travis.

"A good shot ain't worth a damn if we can't see anything and have no food to eat," Calvin said.

"He's right," Tammy said.

"No one asked you who's right and who's wrong!" James said.

"Don't you dare snap at me like that, James Millworth. I'm just calling it how I see it," Tammy said.

"It don't matter how you see it," James said.

Travis looked at his father but saw no sign he'd get between his wife and uncle. Their animosity towards each other had been building for years, and maybe *this* would be their breaking point.

"Sure does in my house," Tammy said.

"Your house? You mean my daddy's house," James said.

"Your *daddy* left it to Cal, not you. If it weren't for Cal, you'd be dead on the street," Tammy said.

"You fuc—"

"Enough, goddammit!" Calvin bellowed this so loud the entire house shook.

"Y'all arguing like this ain't gonna get us anywhere. For Christ's sake, from now on, everyone under this roof does as I say, and if they don't, they can go out there and figure it out for themselves. I hope that's clear because you all know damn well I mean it. Trav, if I say you need to stay awake all night to guard the house, that means you stay awake all night and guard the house. John, if I say you need to help out with supplies to stay here, then you need to help out with supplies to stay here. That all clear?"

Too frightened to look Calvin in the eye, everyone nodded and fixed their gaze on their plate. Calvin cursed at them some more and then grabbed a beer. He stormed off to his bedroom and slammed the door. Travis met James' stare. A couple of days ago, he would've been scared of his uncle being this mad at him, but not anymore.

"Quit it, you two, and eat your damn food. This better be the last breakfast like this, or else no one else is eating breakfast for a long time. Hope that's understood," Tammy said.

"Yes, Ma."

Being there when Luke woke up from a nap was Travis' favorite part of being his uncle. Each time was as though he was seeing the world for the first time. His eyes would open wide and study everything around him. Travis liked to think he was watching his nephew's brain process his surroundings in real time. He couldn't talk, but his expressions were telling. Travis knew how observant and smart he was just by looking at him. That was part of the reason he and Terryn wanted Luke to grow up elsewhere. Who Luke would grow up to be if he stayed around Calvin and James was one of their biggest fears. Terryn cried about it often. Travis told her he was smart enough not to become like their father or uncle, but that never made her feel better.

He and Terryn were kneeling down on opposite

sides of the bed, watching Luke take in the world. Travis was jealous of his nephew. Luke didn't have the slightest idea they were fighting for their lives. His existence was so simple. He wouldn't remember any of *this*, and for that, Travis was grateful.

"So, sounds like everyone is getting along just fine out there," Terryn said.

"Yeah. You could say that," Travis said.

Terryn chuckled and shook her head. Their family underestimated her because of her mistakes, but Travis knew Terryn was much smarter than they gave her credit.

"Why is Pa letting John stay here?" she asked.

"Don't know, but he better start helping, else Pa might throw him out there."

"Hopefully with James."

"Don't think we'll get that lucky."

Luke giggled as if he understood who they were talking about.

"I know, we don't like James," Terryn said in her baby voice.

Luke was a good reminder life was worth living. They just had to make sure his was, too.

"But seriously, Trav. John being here is only going to make things worse. Another mouth to feed, another drunk, another person for James to share his crazy theories with."

"Terryn."

"Oh, stop. They can't hear me."

Travis dropped his chin to his chest and asked, "What do you want me to do about it?"

"Not what I want *you* to do about it. It's what are

we going to do about it."

"How many times do I have to tell you how bad it is out there? I took my mask off for a second last night and thought I was gonna die. And *he* would die out there."

"Don't say th—"

"It's the truth, Terryn. Just 'cause you're ready to leave and would make it, doesn't mean he can. I told you, we have to be patient."

"For how much longer, Trav? 'Cause I can't take it anymore. We're all cooped up in here thinking we're under attack. Sooner or later, we're all gonna go nuts and something's gonna happen. Don't know what it'll be, but something, Trav. You know it won't be good now that James has a friend here.

"I swear to God I could kill him and not reg—"

"Terryn."

Travis saw the anger in her eyes. Neither of them would lose sleep over their uncle's death, but Travis had never thought Terryn could take care of it herself.

"You have to calm down. It's not good for Luke," Travis said.

"Know what's not good for Luke? Living under this damn roof with that maniac and a grandpa and grandma who don't give a damn about him. That's what's not good for Luke, Trav. We gotta get the hell outta here. If we don't soon, it's gonna be too late. I promise you that."

"What do you mean?"

"What I mean is if we stay much longer, we'll never be able to get out."

Travis rubbed his temples and closed his eyes. After

the night and morning he'd had, the last thing he had the energy for was to talk down Terryn. She didn't know what it was like out there, and he did. Just the thought of taking Luke out there gave him the chills.

"Come here," he said.

Terryn picked Luke up off the bed and followed Travis to their bedroom window.

"What do you see out there?" he asked.

Terryn shrugged and said, "Nothing."

"Exactly. It could be like that for hundreds of miles, all right? Imagine going hundreds of miles with Luke and not being able to see or breathe."

Terryn's expression was one of defeat. She said, "I think that's him, Trav. I swear."

"You think what's him?"

"John. That's him, Trav."

Travis pressed his eyes together and looked back and forth at his sister and Luke. Terryn nodded and wiped her tears.

Their father yelled for Travis from the family room.

"Coming," he said.

He kissed Terryn on the cheek and promised her he'd figure out something.

Chapter 5

Night 2 Journal

I'm still not sure if I believe Terryn. Maybe she's telling the truth, but she could be saying whatever will help her get her way. I'd hope she wouldn't do that, but she's lied before. It made me think of when she told me she was having Luke but wouldn't tell Ma and Pa and told me not to tell them either. She must've kept Luke a secret for most of the time she was pregnant. I guess she was lucky she was pregnant when it was cold because she could easily cover up her belly, but keeping him a secret didn't do any of us any good. I'll never forget what happened the night she finally did tell Ma and Pa. That was the scaredest I've ever been. I was scareder that night than I am now.

Pa told me I have to go to town to John's place with John tomorrow. He said if I want to be considered a man, I have to show him I can do things a man does. I wanted to ask him what James is then if he doesn't do anything, but I was too scared. Pa was pissed off anyways, and I didn't want to piss him off anymore. John looked more scared than me when Pa told us that was what we had to do. John tried to act like he wasn't, but I saw it in his eyes. He's definitely more scared than me.

I got lucky, Terryn was asleep when I got back to our room. I wouldn't want to tell her what I have to do tomorrow. It would upset her. She'd probably have one of her fits that makes her so hard to be around sometimes. Pa told us he needs John and me to get to town because he wants to know what other people are doing. He also told us if we see something we need that's not at John's, we need to take it. I'm not sure what he expects us to find when we can't see anything, but maybe we'll know when we get there. Now that I think about it, I'm sure some people have already gone to town and stole some things, but tomorrow's only the third day of this. Maybe people are still too scared to leave their houses or don't have ways to make it there with ash all over the ground. Maybe Pa's too scared to leave the house, and that's why he's sending me and John out there.

Just watching the house last night wasn't as scary as I thought it'd be. How quiet it was scared me at first, but after a while I told myself there couldn't be anything out there that didn't feel scared too. I'm definitely scared about what it'll be like when I have to leave tomorrow. Outside doesn't look like it's any better than it was last night. I was outside so I could help Pa get set up for his watch tonight and still couldn't see very far out in front of me. The ash and smoke are still so bad he won't be able to see whatever's coming before it gets him, but I guess having someone out there watching the house is better than nothing. Pa is good with a gun, though, maybe the best in Stanley. If we are attacked, he's the best person to fight them off.

James told John and me if we see anyone tomorrow and don't shoot first, they will. He makes it sound like it'll be easy, but I think it's easy when you're not the one out there doing the shooting. There's no way James has ever shot anyone in his life. I've seen him with a gun, and I think I'm better. The longer we're locked up in this house with him, the more I hate him. I sort of wish whatever is out there comes and gets him and leaves the rest of us alone. The world would be a better place without him.

I thought James could be Luke's dad for a long time. All the beer he drinks makes him do weird things, and Terryn hates him so much. I thought maybe that was why. There was this one time I saw him sitting next to her and something about it didn't feel right, but maybe I thought that just because I hate him. I've always shared a room with Terryn, and that's why she tells me so much, but maybe that would've been so bad she wouldn't want to tell me. I don't really know. I just wish he was dead. If we ever found out he was Luke's dad, Pa would finally kick him out of the house. He'd have nowhere to go and probably would die. I don't even think Pa would miss him.

I gave up trying to go to sleep. I want to, but I'm thinking about too much stuff. I thought about going outside to keep Pa company, but I don't want to leave Terryn alone, with James and John still awake. I hear them drinking beer and sounding stupid on the couch. I just looked at Terryn and Luke, and they're out cold. Terryn wouldn't stand a chance against them. I think what I'm most scared of is if something happens to me tomorrow, Terryn isn't going to have anyone to help her. Not even Ma helps her out with Luke that much, and I don't think Pa even wants them living here. That's scaring me a lot more than whatever is out there. Even though I'm younger than her, I'm the only person that helps her. Sometimes that scares me, but I'm happy she has me here. I just wish that she'd have some more sense, though. Sometimes she brings trouble in on herself.

I think we have enough supplies in the closet for now, but we'll need a lot more when we escape. If it was up to Terryn, we'd already be gone. I think I could even wake her up right now to go and she'd get ready. I know how much she wants to get out of here, but she doesn't know what it's like out there. I think about leaving Stanley a lot more than Terryn thinks I do. Sometimes she's gotten so mad at me she says I don't have the balls to leave, but that's not true. I just don't know what we'd do out there. I'm not old enough to get a real job, and Terryn has never worked a real job in her life. I'm not sure if she doesn't understand that or if she's just so desperate to leave, she'd do anything.

Right now, though, I should be thinking about tomorrow. John and I will have our guns, but we don't know what other people have out there. Besides, I've never shot at anybody in my life, and I don't know if I can. If anything James says is true, we don't have a chance with just guns anyways. He makes it sound like whatever's out there has superpowers. If they do, tonight will be my last night at home.

Chapter 6

Travis forced himself upright and rubbed his eyes when he heard a loud knock on his door and his father telling him to get up. He'd do anything for more sleep, but it was too late for that now. He stood up and got changed, his anxiousness already kicking in. Tammy opened the door while Travis was putting on his boots and Terryn was changing Luke's diaper.

"Here. One thing you'll be damn sure you're going to do before you go out there is eat something," Tammy said.

His mother handed him the plate and pointed at it. "Eat it now."

"Yes, Ma."

"Dammit, Travis, get in here!" Calvin yelled.

"He's eating something," Tammy said.

"We eat breakfast in the damn kitchen," Calvin said.

Tammy looked at Travis and nodded towards the kitchen. Travis set the plate of eggs, sausage links, and toast on the dresser and told Terryn to eat it.

The tension was palpable at the breakfast table. John's fork trembled every bite he took. Calvin had heavy bags under his eyes. Travis guessed he must've taken his mask off a few times the night before, because ash smeared his cheeks. James was washing down his extra serving of eggs, sausage links, and toast with a Miller Lite. Travis felt his uncle staring at him, but when he stared back, James pretended he wasn't.

"How was it out there last night?" Travis asked.

"Smokey," Calvin said.

"Did you see or hear anything?"

Calvin shook his head and stuffed his mouth with eggs. Travis had seen his father exhausted after a long day of hard work plenty of times, but the look in his eyes this morning was one he'd never seen before; he had aged overnight, and not just because of the heavy bags under his eyes. For the first time, Travis noticed crow's feet on the outer corners of his eyes, worry lines in his forehead so deep, Travis imagined being able to slip a playing card between them.

"After both of y'all finish your breakfast, go to town and then John's. There I want y'all to see if anyone's around and find out if they know anything," Calvin said.

"Okay. Like what?" Travis asked.

"Anything. Like what the hell is going on with all this damn smoke and ash outside."

James found amusement in Calvin raising his voice at Travis.

"Keep that laughter to yourself 'less you want to go with 'em," Calvin told his brother.

"You know you need someone here to help you watch the house," James said.

"You got that right. I'm just not sure if that someone is you."

Travis looked down to hide his smile.

"Like I was saying, when you go to town, find out anything you can. If y'all see anything that might be useful for us, then take it. I hope I don't have to tell you what anything that might be useful for us is. If you don't find anything, that's fine too, because John said he has plenty at his place. Y'all can stop there on your way back and grab what we need. Least John can do to show his thanks for us keeping him company. That right, John?"

"Oh, yeah, I've-I've got plenty Trav and I can get."

"Good. Once y'all are both finished eating, grab some guns and get outta here. I know it's early, but best to leave as soon as possible so you're back by dark," Calvin said.

Chapter 7

Highway 75 ran along the Salmon River and was the only road that led them to town. Typically there were workers' trucks, livestock trailers, and campers racing by, but today there were none. Travis imagined what the campers at the nearby Salmon River, Casino Creek, and Mormon Bend campsites were doing. Those sites were right next to the river, but Travis couldn't imagine that would do them any good at this point. Hopefully, they found refuge somewhere before it was too late.

Travis told himself to quit thinking about things that didn't matter. Not being able to see more than a few feet in front of him was enough to worry about. John stayed within an arm's length of Travis as they muscled through the knee-high ash and rocks. A trigger-happy John being so close worried Travis. He feared John might do something brash—something that would lead to more trouble.

A gunshot rang from what sounded west of them. Travis tensed and steadied his rifle. John nearly jumped out of his shoes and aimed his rifle around wildly.

"Careful with that. Might just be someone killin' breakfast," Travis said.

"Could also be them," John said.

"Could be, but we don't know."

They continued southwest on the highway in silence. Travis' thoughts were racing about what Terryn said. Part of him believed her. Here was a man who sought refuge at their house when he had one of his own. Maybe to be closer to her and his son. He and James getting along so well made Travis more wary, but, Travis reminded himself, Terryn wasn't known for her honesty.

"How much farther you think until we hit town?" Travis asked.

"Dunno. I can't tell with all this smoke and ash. Feels like a while, though."

Travis rolled his eyes.

"How long have you been preppin'?" Travis asked.

"Oh, boy. Lot longer than you've been alive. How old are you now, Trav?"

"Fifteen."

John chuckled and said, "About three times longer than you've been alive."

Yet here he was shaking with fear. Travis saw the rifle trembling in his hands. There was no way he could hit anything right now. He and James being friends made even more sense. Each talked a big game, but both were useless.

Travis let the silence wash over them again as they continued down the highway. Since the gunshot, all they heard was the wind howling, ash flying against their mask and forcing them to stop every few steps. The wind was so strong, forward progress was hard to come by. John complained about the struggle aloud, but Travis paid him no heed. Travis planned to tell his father how much of a coward John was when they got home. Maybe that would be enough for Calvin to send John packing. If they were really lucky, James would go with him.

Travis had little sense of how long or far they'd walked. The poor visibility, wind, ash, and rock made Travis feel they were walking in place. For all he knew, maybe they were. John was so close to Travis now, they were almost shoulder to shoulder. Another gunshot rang, but this time from the north—where home was.

"Hell you think that was?" John asked.

"Someone trying to shoot something or someone," Travis said.

"We should get back to see if they need our help.

Sounded like it was coming from home."

"We will, after we stop in town and your place. If that was at *home*, we don't have to worry. Pa's the best shot in Stanley."

"Not sure if stopping at my place is worth it," John said.

"Why not?"

"Town might have what we need, and if that shot came from your property, it's best we get back as soon as possible. Don't matter how good your daddy's shot is. Their guns are bigger than ours."

"Pa said to stop at your place, John. That's what we're gonna do."

John muttered something under his breath. Travis ignored him. John being too scared to say something aloud said enough.

The smoke became thicker and wind stronger the longer they were out there. The wind blew so hard they had to turn their backs and let it pass at certain points. When the wind finally died down some, Travis checked on John. He was kneeling and had his chin pressed against and arms crossed over his chest.

"It stopped. Let's go," Travis said.

"Not sure we can. Might have to turn around and tell your daddy the conditions got to be too much," John said.

Travis grabbed the back of his shirt and tossed him on his back. He stood over John and crouched so low their masks were nearly touching.

"We're here to do what my daddy told us to do. Now let's go," Travis said.

Without another word, Travis stood up and

continued walking. He didn't fear having his back to John. He heard John get up in a hurry to catch up to him. When he did catch up, he said nothing. Only followed.

They experienced more of the same for the next half hour or so, until they hit a spot on the highway where the ash and rock leveled out. No longer were they up to their knees. Once they could walk more effortlessly, they both realized the beating their legs had taken. There wasn't as much ash on the ground, but it swirled in the air, making the smoke look heavy and suffocating. Travis thought the smoke looked like evil rain clouds hovering over the earth. But instead of watering the earth, they were slowly burning it. A few animal carcasses lay on the road. Some were easy to make out, like the couple of elk they saw, but others were too mutilated to know what they'd been.

A sign for a gas station a mile away appeared out of the smoke. Travis had no idea how many miles they'd already walked for, but a mile to some civilization—or what once was—didn't seem so bad. Travis picked up the pace. John struggled to keep up but had no other choice.

They'd walked, Travis guessed, half a mile since the sign when they saw the flashing yellow lights through the smoke and ash. They tensed up but continued towards them. Neither knew what they might have to shoot, but both were ready.

"Hey, slow down, will ya? That's them," John said.

"We don't know that yet. Could be help," Travis said.

"Anyone 'round here who'd be help wouldn't be

flashin' yellow lights like that, boy."

Now wasn't the time to put John in his place. The potential trouble ahead was far more important.

"Just be careful, all right? You could be right, but we still don't know," Travis said.

Travis and John were now close enough they could hear voices. One was muffled and sounded as if it came from a radio or walkie talkie. The other was from a man who sounded close to the yellow lights. He said he was having a hard time finding good reception. Travis couldn't hear every word, but he got the gist of it: this man was also out there fighting for his life. But whose side he was on was unclear. Travis stuck out his arm and put it on John's chest. The man sounded nearby. Neither Travis nor John knew if he could see them.

Travis got John's attention and lifted a finger to his mouth. John nodded and they slowly approached the lights. The man was leaning into a plow truck. He looked as if he was digging through the middle console. They heard the radio's static from inside the truck. The worsening reception drowned out the faint voice through the radio. The man grunted and cursed as he dug through the middle console. Clearly something had gone awry. You're not alone there, Travis thought.

"Step away from the truck and put your fuckin' hands up!"

John charged the man so fast Travis barely had time to process what happened. In an instant, John's rifle was on the back of the man's head.

"I said step away from the truck!" John said.

"John, what the he—"

John kicked the back of the man's knees so hard,

Travis thought he'd snapped each leg in two. The man still hadn't turned around. Half of him was still in the truck when John grabbed the back of his shirt and threw him backward. His body smacked against the pavement. He had no time to gather himself before John was above him with his rifle at the man's throat.

Travis studied the man. He wore a highlighter yellow jacket with a few silverish stripes going across it. His pants and boots resembled snow gear, and like them, he wore a mask. Travis looked for something that signified who he was but found nothing.

"Please—please. I'm not here to hurt you. I'm here to help, all right?"

"Bullshit. Where's your gun?"

Travis pleaded, "John, get off him. Let him speak for himself before you—"

"Oh, shut the hell up, would ya? I'm tired of hearin' it. It was up to you, he would've already killed us."

"I swear I'm not here to hurt you. I'm here to hel —"

John put a bullet in his throat before he could finish.

"Jesus Christ, John. What was that for? He didn't do anything!" Travis said.

"You keep talkin' to me like that and you'll be next, hear me, boy? Your uncle and I tried tellin' you they're coming. No one wanted to listen. Hell, you still don't. Believe me when I say your daddy would've done the same."

Travis rushed over to the man and knelt next to him.

"I shot him good, boy."

"He could've helped us!" Travis said.

"He also could've been one of 'em attacking us.

146

Stop actin' like you know what the hell you're talkin' about. Maybe then you'll actually learn somethin'."

Travis shook his head. "I don't know why Pa let you in. He should've sent you right back to where you came from. We know you don't have shit. That's why you came to our place. Not fooling anyone."

John steadied his rifle at Travis. He was close enough for Travis to see the menacing look in his eyes. Killing brought something out in John that wasn't there moments ago. Travis had no doubt John was enjoying this, which only gave Travis more reason to fear for his life. The sudden power shift made it hard to believe Travis had been the one leading them up to this point. Killing provided John some sort of satisfaction. Maybe killing people as helpless as the dead man and Travis got him off. Travis would never know for sure, nor did he care to right now. He just didn't want to die, especially at the hands of someone as pathetic as John Patterson.

The next shot rang so loud, Travis briefly lost his hearing. For a moment, he thought that was it. That John Patterson had killed him—that he had taken his last breath.

But when Travis looked up, he saw it was John who had taken his last breath. John's neck went limp a split second before falling backward. His skull smacked the pavement so hard, Travis was sure it cracked.

"You all right?"

The voice came from behind Travis. He turned around and saw a man dressed exactly the same as the man John had killed. He placed his pistol in his holster and put his hands up. He told Travis everything was okay now, that he was safe. He approached the man John had killed and tried to find a pulse. He quickly realized it was useless.

"I'm sorry," Travis said.

"It's not your fault," he said.

"Was he your friend?"

He shook his head and said, "My brother."

Travis felt like crying for him but remembered it would show weakness.

He nodded towards John and said, "Who was he to you?"

"My uncle's idiot friend who was staying with us after we got attacked."

"Attacked?"

"Uh—yeah."

"Who attacked you?"

"I don't know. Whoever did all this," Travis said.

John's killer let out an odd sound from deep in his throat. "No one attacked us, kid. A volcano erupted."

"A volcano erupted?"

"Yeah. This man told you we were under attack?"

Travis nodded. "And my uncle."

"Your uncle as trigger-happy as this man was?"

"What do you mean?"

"Is your uncle as quick to shoot someone as this man was?"

"Maybe he'd try, but he can't shoot for shit."

He chuckled and said, "I like you, kid. What's your name?"

"Travis."

"How old are you, Travis?"

"Fifteen."

"Fifteen. Who sent you out here?"

"My pa."

"And where's he?"

"At home."

"Why did he send you?"

"To head into town and see how everyone else is doing. Then we were supposed to go to John's place and get more supplies, but I don't think he had much to offer. Probably why he came to our house in the first place."

"Is that John?"

Travis nodded.

"If your father really wanted to help your family, he would've come out here himself. It should be him, not you."

Travis could no longer hold back his tears. This man had just lost his brother, but Travis was the one crying. He was waiting to be told to snap out of it. Instead, John's killer knelt beside him and promised he was safe now. Travis collapsed against him and hugged his savior tighter than he'd hugged anyone before. He stayed in his arms and sobbed for a while before the man said, "I'll make sure you'll be all right, kid. I promise you that."

Chapter 8

Journal Entry
4 Months Later

Today was one of the hardest days since we've been here. That shouldn't surprise me though because most days are harder than the last. It's been that way since we got here. I think I hurt my shoulder moving feed today. I didn't want to let Dale know that, though. It wouldn't get me a day off or anything. He'd just tell me to suck it up. Maybe if I was lucky, he'd let me ice it or something before finishing my chores.

We started the day before the sun came up today. If I had to guess, it was probably about 4:00, but I can't be sure. The only clocks here are in Dale's house. He told us time is something we don't need to worry about anymore. There are bigger things we need to worry about, like making it to tomorrow. Every day's mission is to make it to tomorrow. That's why our work will never be done.

Even Dale agreed it's gotten too cold to exercise outside. He let us exercise in the barn this morning, but he said if one person doesn't give their full effort, we'll be back out in the cold doing jumping jacks and pushups until we throw up. He says our normal exercises aren't a punishment. He says we have to do them if we want to see tomorrow. Dale tells us about all the other threats that could be out there. He doesn't really say more than that, but we all listen to him. He knows more than we do.

I think four guys threw up during our exercise this morning. The barn doesn't have heat or anything. It's still pretty cold in there that early in the morning. I don't think it matters where you are at four in the morning. It will always be cold.

After exercise, we had a little breakfast. Just hardboiled eggs today, and then we had class. Today we learned about harvesting all year long. Dale promised us that people who think they can only grow certain foods during certain parts of the year just aren't good at it. I believe him because I remember Ma was always having trouble growing fruits and vegetables no matter what season it was. Pa said he could've done it, but I don't remember him trying to help her. Instead, him and James would just tell her how useless she was.

Dale's way better at harvesting than Ma, Pa, and James ever were. We helped him turn five empty stables into an indoor garden. We knocked down the walls between them and planted rows of fruits and vegetables with walkways, too. That way, we can go and pick them without stepping on any of the plants. The hardest part about it was replacing the roof. Now it's clear, so that if the sun does come out, the fruits and vegetables will get some. We were actually in there today during our class. The plants haven't grown much yet, but Dale said it's just going to take time. He told us he thinks a lot will grow.

Most guys think harvesting is boring and that it's only meant for women. One of them made a joke during one of Dale's harvesting lessons. He said something like, "You can do women's work while I go hunt." Dale slapped him across the face so hard he bled and cried. Ever since that happened, no one has talked to Dale like that. I actually like harvesting, but I don't tell the other guys that. I'd probably end up getting laughed at if they found out. I never realized how important and hard it was when I was still living at home. It makes me feel bad Ma had to do it all on her own.

After our harvesting lesson, we went over what

we have to do to be ready for spring. The seasons aren't what they used to be. Dale says that means we have to make sure we're ready for whatever spring will be. Dale says it might just stay like this forever. There isn't ash up to our knees anymore, but when you're outside, you can tell it was there. Dale doesn't think the world will ever look the same, and I agree with him. When the day's clear enough, we can see a road from Dale's property, but no one is ever on it. I don't think anyone has seen a car drive by since we've lived here. Some guys say that's because people only drive at night because traveling during the day is too dangerous. That doesn't make sense to me. I just think people are too scared to leave their house because they think they won't be able to get back.

Sometimes I feel we're the only people left in the world. Maybe that's why Dale is so hard on us. Maybe he knows we only have each other left. Some of the guys don't take him as seriously as me, but I don't care what they think. I know what happens to people who don't prep right. I'm not going to be one of them.

After we finished up in the slaughterhouse tonight, Sam told me in our room Dale isn't who he says he is. Sam says Dale likes kids more than adults. He says Dale just wants to make it seem like he's helping us, but we're the ones actually helping Dale. I don't really believe Sam, but I've been up all night thinking about what he said. Ever since we went to the house to get Terryn and Luke after Dale killed John, I haven't seen another adult. Me, Terryn, and Luke were the first ones here. A lot of times during our first week here, Dale would leave and come back with more kids like us. It was cool at first because I've never been allowed to hang out with other kids my age. It does seem like having some more adults who know how to prep would help, but maybe there are no more other adults.

Sam told me his daddy was outside when the eruption happened and never came back. His mom shot herself in the mouth at the kitchen table after Sam went to bed the first night. He told me what it was like to wake up the next morning and see her. Some nights he has nightmares and cries and yells in his sleep. I used to think I should wake him up to tell him it's okay, but I've learned just to let it pass. He said when Dale came, he had been out of food for almost two days. That's why he had no problem leaving with Dale, but I think he wishes he'd just stayed home and tried to figure it out by himself. He'd probably be dead too, if he had.

Other kids have said Dale kidnapped them and that their parents were taking care of them. A lot of preppers in Stanley know what they're doing, so I believe some of the kids. I just don't know why their parents wouldn't try to come and get them then. I still think Dale is good, no matter what some of the other guys say. He saved my life, and Terryn's and Luke's life too. John might've killed me if it weren't for Dale. James might've gone crazy and killed Terryn and Luke if Dale hadn't killed him first. Ma and Pa didn't know how to take care of us, either. We would've never made it out of *this* living with them. We already knew we were short on food the day of the eruption. I'm thankful for Dale. He's done a lot for us. He even lets Terryn and Luke sleep in the house. They're the only ones who are allowed to.

Now that I think about it though, Terryn doesn't seem to like living there as much as she did at first. I usually only see her during meals, but a couple days ago I saw her when we were both doing chores in the barn. She looked scared and told me something weird happened the night before. She woke in the middle of the night to take care of Luke because he wasn't feeling good, and heard weird noises coming from Dale's room. She said it sounded like someone was crying. When she went out in the hallway to see if everything was okay, two guys were leaving his room. She didn't see their faces but said she for sure heard them crying. Maybe they did something wrong and were getting yelled at, but Terryn thinks something else was happening. She didn't tell me what, though.

All I know is that I just need to keep doing what Dale tells me to do, so I don't get in trouble. I'm also a little scared about doing something wrong because then, maybe Dale would hurt Terryn and Luke instead of me. I'm just going to keep working hard so none of us get in trouble. I'm going to try to go to sleep now because I already know tomorrow is going to be harder than today. Who knows what will happen to us.

White River National Forest, Colorado

Emily and Simon

by Guy Thair

Nearest town: Meeker
Distance from eruption: 480 miles

Emily sat down at the small table by the window and opened her diary.

She ruled a margin on a fresh page, just as they'd been shown at school (Emily had always considered this a waste of good writing space), then carefully printed and underlined the heading before adding a private running joke.

WEDNESDAY (maybe)

"Ha." The sound, which might once have been mistaken for a laugh had it contained any humor at all, was now just as much a habit as the guesstimated dates in her diary, a reflex, nothing more.

She paused for a moment, glanced over at the figure in the cabin's double bed, listened to the harsh but steady breathing, then wrote:

Today I learned The Man With No Face is called Simon

Emily looked out at the gray landscape, the unchanging, dead blanket of ash stretching away down the hillside towards the lake until it was indistinguishable from the smog of volcanic particles hanging in the air. Her world had shrunk to a circle of perhaps a half-mile radius, although that might as well be reduced further to the size of her father's hunting cabin, since who in their right mind would want to go outside?

Reading back the first line, Emily absently chewed the end of her pencil in thought and continued writing:

I don't know who was more surprised when he spoke for the first time, him or me; maybe he wasn't expecting his voice to work anymore. Or it could have been me; I did shriek, just a little. Maybe I just made him jump.

Simon is sleeping again now. I think the pain is tiring him out. I will make sure not to wake him.

Emily laid down her pencil, sat back in her father's swivel chair, and once more gazed through the window.

However hard she tried, she could not help being drawn back to that view outside, to the frightening gloom of permanent dusk which passed for daylight these days. So much so, she had eventually given up resisting two days ago and moved her writing table here from the opposite corner, as she would only find herself getting up and walking across to the window every few minutes. This way, she at least felt more comfortable, less anxious, somehow.

But, as was so often the case in the last few weeks, she needed distractions or her memory replayed events she really wished she could forget. Emily had taught her mind to swerve away from things like the image of her father telling her it was important she stay inside until he came back because that just led to thinking about him *not* coming back, and *that* led to thinking about what had happened to mom when the car crashed. Or when a great big bear with a broken leg and all the fur burnt off its back had made that horrible noise outside the door all night. Emily had really thought she would be eaten alive, like Goldilocks.

Of course she knew Goldilocks wasn't actually eaten, but she couldn't help thinking a post-apocalyptic reboot might take the story in a very different direction.

Being thirteen was hard enough without all the grown-up stuff Emily had done recently; lighting the fire, learning how the generator worked, cooking her own meals, sending out and listening for messages on the radio. There were so many things to remember.

And all that was before The Man With No Fa... before Simon arrived, she corrected herself, turning once more to study the silently sleeping figure.

No change there, just the imperceptible rise and fall of his chest beneath the blanket, nothing else since they first spoke this afternoon. Still, even that was a huge improvement on the state he was in when he got here, Emily thought, as her mind drifted back to that horrifying night... was it only a week ago?

It might have only been seven days earlier, but a totally different girl sat alone in the cabin on that (maybe) Wednesday evening. Still fragile, still in shock, less hardened as yet to the harsh new realities of life, Emily was crying.

She burst into tears at some strange times, as well as the more understandable bedtimes, mealtimes, and first thing in the mornings. Yesterday afternoon she'd sobbed uncontrollably for a full fifteen minutes while sitting on the toilet, tears and snot dripping onto the floor between her pink trainers, all because Emily had remembered that Tigger, the family cat back home in Denver, was almost certainly dead by now.

But she'd pulled herself together, carefully wiped the floor clean and got on with something, anything to take her mind off, well, everything else.

She had just finished her daily routine of sweeping the floor, getting the fire ready in the wood-burning stove, checking the fuel level in the generator and was deciding what she would have for dinner that evening, when she thought she heard a noise outside.

Emily froze. Had the bear come back, madder and hungrier than before? She listened, straining to make out anything over the pounding of the blood in her ears, then there it was again.

A slow, heavy scraping sound, as though something

was being dragged along the rough wooden boards of the porch.

The sound stopped and Emily held her breath for what seemed like forever, then let it out again in an involuntary yelp as the door rattled in its frame.

The sudden shock broke the spell and she practically threw herself across the room, slammed the heavy bolt into place and rushed over to the fireplace, where she grabbed the iron poker and raised it like a sword in front of her, facing the now silent front door.

After standing there for a minute or two with no noises from outside, Emily, feeling faintly ridiculous, lowered the poker but kept a firm hold on it as she tiptoed over to the window by the door and peered round the edge of the curtains.

She frowned as she tried to work out what she was looking at, had someone wrapped a lump of barbequed meat in a dirty rag and dumped it on the porch?

But something about the shape of ... wait, were those toes?

"Eeewww!" Emily recoiled from the window, nearly dropping the poker.

Her hand caught up with her ears and clapped itself over her mouth as she listened intently, staring at the door. Then her brain took a quick diversion and she was briefly certain the cabin was about to be invaded by zombies. Emily regained what was left of her composure, crept back to the window and pressed her cheek against the warm glass to get a better view of ... whoever it was.

Now that the initial shock had worn off, she could tell the foot she'd seen was more blackened by dirt and ash than actually burned, although the sole was covered with cuts and angry-looking red blisters, as was its partner, which was also partially visible.

Whoever the owner of the damaged feet was, wasn't moving anymore and Emily wouldn't learn anything else from here, so she moved to the door. Leaning the poker against the frame, she took hold of the iron bolt above the handle and, as silently as she could, slid it back until it cleared its keep, picked up the poker again, and grasped the door handle tight. Raising the makeshift weapon over her head, Emily, not giving herself time to think, yanked down on the handle and pulled the door towards her in one rapid movement.

Which was when the man, having fallen against the door when his strength finally gave out, collapsed once again, this time onto the floor of the cabin at Emily's feet.

This time she shrieked more than just a little. It was obvious from his lack of reaction that her uninvited guest was not troubled by the noise or the poker hovering unsteadily over his head for that matter, so Emily lowered it cautiously and leaned over to get a closer look.

His position on the floor meant his head was turned away from her, face obscured by the hood of a torn, ash-covered pale blue sweatshirt, USGS printed on the back in large white letters and, smaller, below it, "Science for a changing world."

"Well, if science wants to make itself useful to the world," said Emily to the hooded stranger, "now would be a good time to start."

She looked through the open doorway for a few

seconds at the forbidding landscape beyond, shivered despite the dry, stifling atmosphere and returned her attention to the new arrival in her shrunken universe.

He wasn't a large man, but Emily knew she would not be strong enough to lift his dead weight on her own, let alone carry him inside, so she looked around the sparsely furnished cabin for inspiration, not wanting the door open any longer than necessary.

Checking the man gave no sign of leaping up and attacking her when her back was turned, she hurried to the room containing the generator, freezer, gun cabinet, her family's baggage and other essential equipment her father kept in the cabin. She opened a wooden chest in the corner and, sure enough, on top of the neatly packed camping gear inside was a folded blue groundsheet, which Emily carried to the front door and unfolded on the floor next to the mystery man, then stood back and tried to work out what to do next.

She would have to roll him over, that was the only way she'd get him onto the shiny plastic sheet, but first, Emily had to make certain he was still alive. After all, she didn't want to go through this whole thing just to discover she was sharing the cabin with a corpse; that wouldn't do at all.

She crouched down at his side, gingerly took his left wrist in a light grip and felt for a pulse. Initially, she really thought he was dead, then after moving her hand a few times and pressing a little harder, she finally detected the faintest of beats beneath her fingertips and sighed in relief as she stood up.

"Ok, you're alive; let's do this."

Emily sounded more determined than she actually

felt, but they had always recited that mantra before soccer practice and it had become a kind of internal catchphrase for her when she lacked confidence or was unsure if she was brave enough to try something new.

Standing on the groundsheet next to him, she braced her right foot against the door frame behind her, reached across his body to grab his right shoulder with both hands, and heaved. Maybe he was lighter than he looked, or maybe Emily was stronger than she'd thought, but the body shifted surprisingly quickly. It caught her off balance as he rolled towards her, toppled her backward onto the hard floorboards and sent a bolt of pain to the top of her head from the jolt to her tailbone.

For a few seconds, Emily couldn't move and was nauseated, only moments away from bursting into tears if she didn't get a grip on herself. She had a sudden thought: what if the act of moving her unconscious visitor had woken him up?

Grabbing the edge of her writing desk for support, she pulled herself to her feet and looked down into his face for the first time.

This time, Emily screamed.

Looking back on it now, a full week (or possibly a lifetime) since it had happened, Emily was still amazed she'd had the presence of mind to step outside onto the porch before she threw up what was left of her lunchtime sandwiches. Shakily, she wiped her mouth with the back of her hand as she dared a brief, horrified glance in his direction, then squeezed her eyes shut and counted to ten as her heart rate gradually returned to normal.

Emily walked back into the cabin without looking down at him; she had to get the door closed before she could deal with that again. She grabbed a dish towel from the kitchen and, without looking directly at the poor man, laid it over his ... his face. Emily told herself, don't think of it as anything else; it's his face.

She moved the dining table against the wall by the stove to create a clear space in line with the door and returned to pick up the corners of the groundsheet. Her trainers provided a good grip on the floor and, with a firm hold of the bunched-up corners, Emily took up the slack; it steadily inched across the floor. Within a few minutes, she had dragged the motionless figure fully inside the cabin, closed and re-bolted the door, before sitting down for a well-earned cry.

"Right, I guess the first thing we need to do is see to your face," said Emily, in a calm, matter-of-fact voice. "We have plenty of bandages in the first aid kit."

Ten minutes later and, after a short bout of helpless sobbing, more a release of tension than anything else, she felt a lot better and ready to take on the next challenge.

Namely, taking a good look at what was under that dish towel and trying to make her guest's awakening as comfortable as possible.

She warmed a pan of water on the stove and collected as many clean towels and washcloths as she could find, all of which she laid out next to The Man

With No Face (as Emily's subconscious insisted on calling him, much to her embarrassment), then she took hold of the dish towel and slowly lifted it away.

Even though she was prepared for the sight of it this time, his face, or what was left of it, made Emily gasp.

"Ooh, you poor man, whatever happened to you?"

The hood had fallen back when she had dragged him into the cabin, revealing he'd lost most of his hair on one side and what there was on the other side was singed and shriveled against the vivid red skin of his scalp.

His forehead was a mass of open wounds, blisters which had burst, exposing the tender raw flesh beneath. His eyelids were horribly blistered and swollen, but otherwise intact, although it was impossible to tell for sure.

But it was his nose and mouth which had sustained the most damage, the reason for which Emily later deduced from the terrible burns on the underside of his right forearm. At some point in his journey to her cabin, he had protected his face from the flames, instinctively throwing up his arm to cover his eyes. The action may well have saved his sight but had cost him the lower half of his face.

Emily used wound cleaner from her minimal stock of medical supplies, squirting the soothing liquid over the most seriously damaged areas to dislodge as much ash and dirt as possible. Wincing as flaps of burnt skin moved under even the softest touch, she gently dabbed the scorched flesh dry with cotton balls, then applied a thin film of antiseptic cream and sterile dressing strips to give him a little more comfort and protection.

Kneeling over the motionless figure, she wrapped his head and feet in rolls of elastic bandage, leaving gaps across his eyes and mouth, before carefully placing a pillow under his head and turning her attention to his arm.

Emily anxiously watched over her patient for the next two days, in between increasingly frequent stints on the radio, trying to reach somebody, anybody, in the outside world who could come to her rescue. But the world remained eerily silent, both here in her small, grey bubble and out there on the airwaves, where she feared nobody heard her calls for help.

It wasn't until the third day that The Man With No Face finally returned from whatever limbo state he had occupied since his arrival, giving Emily the second biggest scare she'd had that week.

She had been going through her daily routine of checking his dressings and patiently dripping water between his ruined lips from a piece of sponge when he suddenly made a loud groaning noise and coughed violently. His head and shoulders jerked a few inches up from the floor before sinking back with another groan.

Water from the cup she was holding splashed onto the blankets as Emily nearly jumped out of her skin with fright, but he showed no other signs of life.

The only visible difference was the more pronounced rise and fall of his chest as he breathed more deeply, which Emily thought must be good, and she felt herself relax just a tiny bit for the first time in what felt like a week.

Over the following couple of hours, she watched him coming slowly back into the world; at least that was how it seemed to her. Even lying down, he'd lost that dead, slumped posture, the subtle flexing of muscles and shifting of limbs already giving his body a more lifelike appearance. But the downside of this, it quickly became obvious, was the return of the pain.

Emily had anticipated this possibility and had made an inventory of all the painkillers in the cabin; there was a bottle of 200 Tylenol tablets in the bathroom cabinet and a half-empty packet of her father's oxycodone back pain medication in the nightstand. Seeing his name on the label brought back the tears and she had sat on the bed until they passed, but Emily knew he'd have been glad they would ease someone else's pain and that somehow made her feel ok.

"Thanks, Dad," she sniffed and stood up. "We could always rely on you to make it better."

She read the information leaflet carefully, even all the scary side effects. She didn't want to kill him with an overdose now she'd nursed him back to life. That really would be unfortunate.

Emily knelt beside him. Just from the way he turned his head towards the sound, she knew he was awake.

"Hello, my name is Emily, can you hear me?" she reached for his hand under the blanket, "Don't try to speak. If you can hear me, squeeze my fingers."

She thought he hadn't heard her at first and was about to ask again when she felt the lightest of pressure on her hand, then again, stronger this time.

"That's good, welcome back. You've been asleep for

nearly three days; I was worried about you."

The grip on her hand tightened as he tried to lift himself up, but he cried out and fell back, coughing again but less harshly than before. Emily gently laid her hand on his chest to prevent him from hurting himself again.

"Just lie still, you've been very poorly and you need to rest." She waited to see if he'd respond and when he didn't she continued. "I have something here for the pain. Do you think you could swallow them with a little water?"

A pause, then that slight pressure on her fingers once more.

"Ok, here's the cup, take a sip. I'll hold it for you." She tipped his head forward with one hand and brought the cup to his damaged lips with the other. "Be careful, your mouth is going to be very sore."

He flinched as cold metal brushed against ragged skin, but took the water gratefully. When he was ready, Emily placed the tablets on his tongue and watched as he swallowed, in case he choked.

"Now you should sleep; you'll feel better when you've rested. You're safe here; I'm not going anywhere."

She was about to pull her hand away and was surprised when he held it there. He turned his face towards her and gave her fingers one more, very definite squeeze, with very definite meaning.

"You're welcome. Now do as you're told and get some sleep. When you wake up and if you're feeling better, I'll see how your eyes are, but best keep them shut for now. I think they might be a bit stuck."

He squeezed her fingers again, but this time he let go and seemed to relax. A few minutes later when his breathing returned to normal and Emily knew he was asleep, she stood up and went to find something for dinner.

Simon

The last thing he remembered was a sudden, ear-splitting roar. Seconds later, the rolling grey cloud was speeding towards the bus, covering the windows, plunging him into darkness.

Jumbled images and sensations.

Falling.

Screams.

Pain.

Then the world went black and silent.

Simon had no way to tell how much later it was. An hour? A day? A week?

Everything hurt. A heavy weight on his legs pinned him down on an uncomfortably warm, smooth metal surface. The air was hot and thick with smoke and suffocating dust. Despite the near-darkness, an unpleasant, sickly orange glow filtered through the murk. As his eyes adjusted to the dim light, he tried to make sense of his surroundings.

It took him a few moments to determine where he was lying — not on the floor as he had originally thought, but on the ceiling of the overturned bus.

"Oh, shit, yeah, we crashed." His voice sounded dead and flat in the choking hot air. He coughed violently, feeling the gritty taste of, what was that, ash?

Cautiously, he pushed himself up on his elbows, lifting his head and shoulders, straining to get a better look at what trapped his legs.

An indistinct, bulky mass, wedged between the luggage racks above each seat, lay across his knees. He grabbed a steel pole to his left and tried to slide himself backward, but he was too firmly stuck. Instead, he took hold of the pole with both hands, one above the other and hauled himself upwards.

Thirty seconds later, worried that either his grip on the pole would give out or his knees would snap first, he gave one more desperate heave, teeth clenched against the pain. He groaned, but the weight suddenly shifted, slipping far enough that he pulled himself free. He collapsed, coughing uncontrollably until he could barely catch his breath.

Spitting out a mixture of ash and bile, he forced himself to breathe as little as possible, made it to his hands and knees and used the pole to get the rest of the way to his feet. Swaying dizzily, he made his way carefully towards the open door at the front of the bus, broken glass crunching under his feet as he held onto the inverted luggage racks for support on the slippery surface.

The door was partially blocked by what was left of the bus driver, who had clearly taken the full force of whatever had blown them off the road. Simon avoided looking too closely as he climbed over the horribly burnt and mangled corpse, but just a brief glimpse and the smell was enough to make him gag.

The world he stumbled into he no longer

recognized, and two things were obvious; firstly, something was very seriously wrong, a lot more serious than a bus wreck; secondly, he didn't think he was going to jail anytime soon.

Simon Morris, sociopath, convicted armed robber and unrepentant cop killer, surveyed the transformed landscape stretching down the hillside into the curtain of smog fifty feet below him and struggled to take in the scale of devastation.

"What the hell happened here? Did they finally drop the bomb on the good ol' US of A?" He laughed bitterly, turned to look at the wrecked bus with the words *Rio Blanco Jail* just visible on the scarred paintwork and saw another body hanging half out of a window, the orange jumpsuit covered in blood and ash.

"Heh, about fucking time someone hit the reset button. We've had it coming, everyone's gone soft, maybe this'll help weed out the damn snowflakes from the patriots once and for all."

Now his mind was clearing. An unpleasant stickiness on his legs made him look down at his own prison overalls. They, too, were soaked in blood from the knees down. It dawned on him that what weighed him down after the crash was the body of one of the two guards accompanying him and his fellow detainee on their way to a lifetime of incarceration. "Hmm, The Man always tryna hold me down, hahaha."

This thought amused him so much he was still chuckling to himself about it when he reached the road five minutes later and almost didn't see the figure running towards him out of the gloom.

"Oh my god, you're alive, I didn't think anyone else made it! Are you hurt?"

Simon thought fast, took in the blue hoodie, jeans and work boots, the fact the newcomer had a similar build to his own, the young man's cracked and ash-smeared glasses.

He made a snap decision and staggered a few steps to the right, dropping to one knee with an apparent cry of pain, his hand resting on a broken, still smoldering branch, head bowed, muscles tensed.

The man in the hoodie ran to his side and reached down to help, too late to realize his mistake as Simon looked up at him and grinned, his arm already swinging the makeshift club in a short, brutal arc.

An hour later, in his newly acquired clothes and boots, a mask fashioned from strips torn off his jumpsuit, Simon pressed on down the mountain road, keeping a wary eye out for any other survivors of what must have been a volcanic eruption of cataclysmic proportions. An educated guess on his part, admittedly, but a pretty safe bet. He had discovered the young man's truck abandoned a couple of miles down the road from the site of the bus crash, *United States Geological Survey* on the side. On the front seat, a briefcase containing files marked *National Geospatial Technical Operations Center (Building 810) - Denver, CO.* The contents were way over Simon's head, but he got the idea well enough.

The files were full of computer printouts

referencing Yellowstone National Park and many graphs with huge spikes in them, dated the same day he'd boarded the bus to jail, suggested he'd been unconscious for at least 24 hours, maybe more. He found a cell phone in the glove box, as dead as the truck's clock, so no help confirming the time or date.

"So the Big One finally blew her top, ain't that a kick in the nuts. Well, bye-bye Wyoming, I guess." Talking to himself always helped focus his thoughts, and gave him direction when he was planning what to do.

"What are we, like, five hundred miles away? Jesus Christ, that must have been some blast, if this is what it's like here, then we're on the edge of the Dead Zone, partner. Ain't nothing going to survive to the north or east of here; they are fucked with a capital F, heh heh. Reckon our luck held out again, we better come up with a good sob story in case we run into anyone on the road."

Simon kept heading down the mountain, occasionally detouring round the wreckage of burned-out vehicles, one with an incinerated body still behind the wheel. As he walked, he concocted a suitably heart-wrenching tale of personal tragedy and was so engrossed in his fictional backstory he only became aware of the sound when it was almost too late. He stopped to listen as he approached a bend in the road, which prevented him seeing more than a hundred yards ahead. Was that the sound of an engine, an aircraft, maybe?

"Ah, no, not that."

Faster than he thought possible, a wall of flame tore

through the trees on the far side of the bend and raced up the side of the road towards him, engulfing everything in its path with a deafening roar of splintering timber.

Simon ran in the only direction he could, back the way he'd come, until he found a place on the other side of the road where he could make his way up the mountainside, away from the flames and into the unknown.

A few hundred yards of battling his way up the overgrown, ash-covered slope, exhausted, fingernails broken and bleeding from the climb, eyes streaming from the smoky air, he had to stop. Overcome by a fit of coughing, he held onto a tree for support until it passed. Adjusting the filthy mask to more tightly cover his nose and mouth, Simon fought to control his breathing, then turned to look back down the mountain as the roar of flames behind him suddenly grew louder.

It had only taken moments for the fire to jump the narrow road to consume the new fuel there, advancing towards him in an unstoppable crackling curtain of death.

He ran, as much as it was possible to run, lungs burning, hands torn to shreds, pulling himself over the uneven ground in a desperate attempt to escape the fire, close to his back now, running for his life.

Until he ran into a wall. Not a wall, on closer inspection, but a rocky outcrop about ten-feet high which blocked his progress completely. He panicked, scrabbling along the rough surface for a handhold, a step, anything to pull himself up and away from the encroaching flames.

He howled in frustration, the heat unbearable, sure his hair would be alight any second, hardly able to breathe. Then his right hand, feeling along the rocky wall in blind desperation, suddenly came up against thin air and he almost lost his balance and fell forward.

What came next happened so fast, Simon didn't work out the precise sequence of events until much later. His survival instinct took over and he acted by reflex, alone.

Before he had a chance to get behind the rock wall for protection, he spun round at an explosive *CRACK* to see a flaming branch falling towards him. Terror took control of Simon's legs, propelling him backward in a stumbling leap, his right arm instinctively warding off the impact.

The weight of the blow knocked him back against the rocks, the sleeve of his sweatshirt burst into flames, the skin of his arm sizzling and blistering on contact. He screamed and desperately clawed his way out from under the fiercely burning log, the rubber soles of his stolen boots smoking, a new agony radiating across his feet from the red hot steel toe caps.

He finally made it round the outcrop, frantically looking for anywhere he could shelter as the roar of the fire rose to a deafening pitch.

Then he saw it, a shallow vertical crevice in the rock no more than two feet deep. A meager sanctuary, but he squeezed himself in, just as another tree crashed down in front of him, showering him in burning debris and setting fire to his hair. Too tightly confined to raise even a hand to extinguish the flames, the pain was so overwhelming he thought he would go insane.

He opened his mouth to scream. The furnace-like air rushed down his throat, robbing him of his voice and igniting his facemask in a bright flare, scorching his eyes and pushing him over the edge into madness even as the darkness rushed to meet him.

Simon Morris surrendered to the nothingness, this time with gratitude, for he was sure this time it was the end.

Another day, another agonized awakening.

The shock of pain when Simon moved the first time, after he regained consciousness, made him pass out after only a few seconds. He had no way to tell how much later it was when he contorted his burnt and battered body enough to free it from the mountain's rocky clutches, nor did he know how he'd squeezed himself into such a tiny space.

His legs gave way as soon as he was free and when he hit the ground, the blackness rolled up in waves, threatening to drag him back under, but he fought against it, channeling the pain into rage and the will to live.

"Survival of the fittest, isn't that what they say?"

He looked up through the blur of ash and pain to see, with very little surprise, a vision of the dead bus driver, sitting on a boulder, charred head tilted grotesquely backward as though searching for something above him, left arm missing at the elbow. His right hand held a cigarette, which he was smoking in an almost comical manner, at least Simon thought so, newly freed from his sanity as he was.

"Hey, watcha doing, sitting there feeling sorry for yerself? Gotta get up and get moving." The driver coughed and spat out a blob of grey phlegm, not seeming to care when it landed in his empty eye socket. "Need to find us somewhere to hole up and gather our strength."

Simon checked his legs for broken bones, miraculously finding none, but noted his boots were ruined, the melted soles hanging off, uppers flapping uselessly around his ankles.

"Come on, don't fuck about. Time to go." The bus driver stood and lurched off up the slope, the back of his head bouncing between his shoulder blades, his upside-down stare still fixed on Simon as he disappeared into the smog.

The broken shell of Simon Morris's mind had cracked wide open, but a dull madness filled the void now and the feeling was almost comforting.

"You know he ain't real, right?"

"Yeah, course I do; I'm not that dumb. But I don't mind the company and he does have a point."

"Right, best get a fucking move on like the man said, hadn't we?"

He made it to a kneeling position, waited for the nausea to pass while peering around him through the shriveled slits of his eyelids, then very carefully stood up. His feet protested in no uncertain terms about their lack of protection, but this was minor compared to the indescribable agony radiating from the horror of his face. It was only that new, quickly expanding, red spark of madness which forced him onward, muttering incoherently to himself as he followed the bubbly, croaking voice of his new friend.

Surrounded by the blackened skeletons of trees, poking through a blanket of ash in all directions, visibility in the smoky, choking air almost zero, Simon walked, staggered and crawled up the mountain for what felt like an eternity. Whenever he stumbled or fell, the exhortations from his undead tour guide spurred him on, not allowing him a moment's rest.

"Quick march, quick march, come on, man, what's the matter with you?"

"What are you doing on your hands and knees? You're not a fucking baby! Get up and walk like a man."

"Won't be long now, you mark my words, just over that next ridge, you'll see…"

So it continued, hour after hour, mile after mile, he trusted in the voice to lead him to safety. Now he was somehow numb to the pain, mental and physical sensory overload had blown all his fuses long ago.

And sure enough, shortly before sundown on the second day, he stepped out of the tree line into a clearing, unburnt this far up the mountainside though still covered with a heavy layer of grey ash. At the center of this oasis of calm stood a cabin.

"Whad'ya know, didn't I say I'd get you fixed up? Man of my word, that's me!"

Simon looked round at the bus driver, who attempted a salute, but realizing his head was elsewhere, made do with a cheery wave instcad.

"Well, you won't be requiring my services anymore.

You're a resourceful fella, I can see that, so I'll be on my way."

Frowning — the expression of a man who knows something isn't right but can't quite put his finger on it — Simon watched the apparition fade back into the shadows of the forest, summoned the last vestiges of strength, and dragged himself the final few yards to the cabin.

The hell of blackness and delirium was almost worse than the pain; he was grateful for the hot needles of agony piercing his flesh during those first few days of semi-consciousness; they honed his senses and kept him sharp. He hid his returning strength from the girl, letting her believe she was dealing with a complete invalid until it was too late.

Now, a week later, he was sure he'd convinced her he wasn't a threat and was finally feeling strong enough to deal with the problem of Emily for good, whenever an opportunity next presented itself.

Emily

"My name is Simon," he stopped and coughed, sipping from the cup of water she handed him, "I work for the US Geological Survey over in Denver." He paused to catch his breath.

"It's alright, take your time." Emily adjusted the pillow behind his head. "Don't try to talk if it's too painful."

Barely an hour since he'd startled her with his first

croaky attempts at speaking, it was getting easier for him all the time. Emily had filled the time telling him how she had come to be alone at the cabin. He had listened, then reached out and squeezed her hand tight and stared at her through the slit in his bandaged face with what Emily imagined was shock and compassion. Later he had even been able, with her help, to reach the bed where she had made him comfortable on a pile of pillows.

Emily was greatly relieved to see her patient making such a speedy recovery and congratulated herself for tending to his injuries so effectively.

Simon swallowed another mouthful of water. "No, it's ok, my throat is just very dry, that's all." He handed the cup to Emily and lay back. "As I said, we were in the truck on the way back from Yellowstone to the USGS office in Denver when the eruption happened–"

"You were *at* Yellowstone?" Emily whispered, eyes wide in awe. "Was it very frightening? Did you see the volcano?"

"Er... no, we, um, we left after taking our readings. We'd been on the road a couple of days before the blast. The rest of the team was killed when we crashed." Simon coughed again, face screwed up in pain. "Sorry, just can't seem to shake this damn cough."

"Oh, Simon, I'm so sorry. That must have been just awful for you."

He smiled weakly. He's trying to be brave, thought Emily, watching him compose himself before he continued. "It was pretty scary, yes, we had no warning at all. The bus was blown right off the road."

"The bus?"

"What?"

"You said the bus was blown off the road. I expect you meant your truck?"

"What, oh, yes, sorry, the truck was blown right into the trees… I was lucky I was thrown clear."

"Yes, that was very lucky," said Emily, frowning. "Were you in the back, then?"

About to speak, a violent bout of coughing overcame Simon, she passed him the water and after a minute or two, he breathed normally again.

"To be honest, I don't know what happened… I just remember waking up in the dark and making the climb up through the woods to the road. I was heading back down the mountain when I got cut off by the flames and that's why I ended up here."

"Didn't you go and check if your friends were ok?"

"Huh? Oh, no, it was obvious nobody was going to get out of that alive. The truck was completely wrecked."

"But they could have been thrown clear like you were, couldn't they?"

"Look, trust me, they didn't make it, ok?"

Now he sounded angry. Emily *knew* something wasn't right, she just didn't know what it was. But her dad always said she was like a dog with a bone; when she put her mind to something, she kept on gnawing until she reached the heart of it.

"Um… didn't you say it was dark? There could have been people who needed your help." A thought occurred to her, "Hey, if we can reach somebody on the radio, we could ask them to check on your friends on the way up here. Do you know how to use one like that?" Emily pointed hopefully to the small radio on the shelf by the bed and he stared at it thoughtfully.

"Well, I'd need to look at it more closely, but I think so. You don't know how to work it?"

"I thought I did, my dad showed me how, but maybe I'm not doing it right, nobody ever replies."

"Perhaps I can fix it if it's not working. I'll take a look tomorrow. I'm feeling quite tired again now, so if you don't mind…"

"Oh, of course, you must be exhausted. I'll let you sleep; there's no rush, you concentrate on getting better."

While he slept, Emily wrote in her diary, gazed out at the ash-covered mountainside and wondered about the niggling little voice in the back of her head, when Simon's voice jarred her back to reality for the second time that day.

"Erm, I wonder if you could–" He sounded almost sheepish. "I mean, I need to use the…"

"Oh! The bathroom? Of course, how stupid of me; I didn't think to ask." Emily was mortified; where were her manners? "I'm *so* sorry, here, let me help you."

Simon laughed at his own awkwardness as Emily waited by the bed for him to swing his feet down onto the floor. He placed his hand on her shoulder to steady himself and stood up, visibly wincing at the stiffness in every muscle and joint, jolts of pain coming from the shredded skin of his bandaged feet.

He was getting back into bed when Emily had a flash of inspiration. "Simon, I know you can't take a shower or anything, but I do have Dad's bags here, I'm sure there's something in there that'll fit you. Wouldn't it be nice to get rid of those nasty burned clothes?"

He seemed about to refuse the offer, but then she saw him glance at the dirty grey patch on the bed sheets and pause before turning back to her with what she guessed was a smile.

"That's very kind, I'd be honored to borrow some of your dad's clothes, thank you, Emily."

"I'll go and find you something. Do you need any help?"

"I should be able to manage the pants on my own, but I think we'll have to cut this off." He pulled at the front of his tattered blue sweatshirt and grinned. "I don't really think it's worth saving, anyway. Um, do you have a towel or something I can wrap around me?"

"Of course, I'll fetch you one. I think we have scissors, too. Just call when you're ready. Take your time; I'll just be out back."

Emily went to her writing table, marked the page in her diary and put it away in the drawer. She brought Simon a towel from the bathroom and headed to the store room to find him something to wear.

Simon

He watched her leave, waited a few seconds until he heard a door open and close, then made straight for the radio by the bed. Picking it up, he resisted the urge to rip the wires from the back and be done with it. He needed more time to think.

What if someone had heard her calling on the radio and couldn't reply? Were they already on the way here right now?

How would he explain the girl's body to a rescue party?

No, he should work out what to do next before making any rash decisions. After all, neither of them were going anywhere, and while he was unable to travel, she was still useful to him.

Glancing at the storeroom door to check it was still closed, he went to the kitchen, took a small paring knife and returned to the radio. He made sure the power was off, then used the knife to remove the screws from the back of the metal cabinet and pulled out the first few wires he found. As the final screw went back into place, Emily called from the back room.

"Are you nearly ready out there? I think I've found a few things that will fit you."

"Yes, won't be long." He took the knife back to the kitchen, then sat on the bed. "These pants are harder to get off than I thought. Give me a couple of minutes."

Simon braced for the pain and forced himself not to curse out loud as he stripped off the torn and bloodstained pants. Waves of agony coursed up his legs as he pulled them over his ruined feet. The ever-present background hum of madness dulled the worst of it, numbing him, pushing the blackness away, clearing his mind. He fell heavily back onto the bed, raised his legs to ease the pain, reached for the towel. Emily called again, concern in her voice. "Are you ok, Simon?"

"Yes, I'm good, you can come in now."

He sat on the edge of the bed, towel wrapped round his legs, doing his best to look friendly and grateful. The floating red mist in front of his eyes faded, clammy sweat cooled beneath the bandages, nothing suspicious or out of place.

Emily held out a pair of grey sweatpants and a zipped red sweatshirt with *San Francisco 49ers* on the back. He nodded his thanks, took them from her, placed them on the bed beside him.

"I thought it would be easier to have one that didn't go over your head." she pointed to the red top and grinned. "I just hope you're a 49ers fan."

Simon picked up the shirt and inspected it with exaggerated care, "Well, I never was much of a sports fan, but in this case I'll make an exception. I'll wear it with pride, thank you."

"Now, let's see about getting those horrid old clothes off, shall we?" Emily picked up a large pair of scissors, making snipping motions in the air and Simon held up his hands in mock terror, making her giggle.

"Ok, you'll have to sit *very* still, I don't want to slice your tummy open."

"No, I'd rather you didn't do that, either. It's ok, I'm kidding, I promise I'll stay still."

Emily slid the long blade under the hem of the smoke-blackened material and carefully began cutting up the front of it, revealing an equally torn and filthy undershirt, which had probably once been white but was now stained with ash and what looked like dried blood.

Once Emily cut through the thick neckline it was easy enough for her to help Simon slide out of the sleeves, taking as much care as possible to avoid damaging the dressing on his badly burned arm.

She stood back and looked at him, frowning. "It's

no good; we can't have you going to bed in that gross undershirt. It's got blood and who knows what else on it. That'll have to come off, too." Trying not to blush, she held out the scissors, "You can do it if you like, I won't look."

He thought for a moment. "I'll tell you what, if I lie down, you can cut it up the back, then I think I can take it off myself, would that be ok?"

Emily nodded gratefully. "Yes, I can do that. Just don't move."

"No, ma'am. I'll not move a muscle til you tell me to, cross my heart and hope to die."

Emily giggled again and started snipping.

Emily

Ten minutes later Simon was tucked up in bed and Emily hadn't even finished clearing up his old clothes when his snoring filled the room. She smiled. It had been a long time since anything made her giggle and it felt nice. Maybe something positive would come from all this horror. Maybe there was light at the end of the tunnel after all.

Emily took a sleeping bag from the camping supplies, left a glass of water and two Tylenol on Simon's bedside table and turned off the light. She settled down on the couch for the best night's sleep she'd had in ages, untroubled by nightmares for the first time since arriving at the cabin.

Simon was already out of bed, stiffly walking back

and forth across the room when she awoke, occasionally stopping to lean on the back of a chair or the kitchen counter to rest.

"Good morning, Emily. Did you sleep well?"

"I did, thank you. You're obviously feeling better this morning. Did you find the painkillers I left for you?"

"Yes, I'm very stiff today, *everything* hurts." He laughed. "But they helped a little. Thanks, that was thoughtful of you."

"Are your bandages still ok? How's your face feel today? It must be very painful."

She stood up as Simon limped over to the couch and leaned on the back of it, looking directly at her from behind his mask of bandages.

"It's a lot less painful than if you hadn't been here to look after me, Emily; I know that for sure. I don't know if I thanked you properly yet, but I just want to say that you might very well have saved my life when you took me in. I am forever in your debt for that. You are a very brave young lady."

She did blush this time, busying herself with her sleeping bag as she replied. "Oh, that's very kind of you, but all I did was bandage you up and hope you didn't die. I was really scared all the time and not at all brave, but thank you."

Emily carried her sleeping bag back to the store room and returned with a trash bag to fill with Simon's ruined clothes when he pointed to the radio.

"So, what seems to be the problem with this, then?"

"Oh, yes, I forgot," Emily put the bag down and walked over to stand next to him. "Well, I *think* everything works; I just don't know if anyone can hear me." She turned on the power to the radio and perched on the edge of the bed. "I can't tell whether it's broken or if there's nobody picking up." She frowned. "That's funny. There should be a little red light at the top there." She tapped a small plastic cover on the corner of the front panel. "It usually comes on with the power."

Emily clicked the switch on the wall socket up and down a couple of times, then took out the plug and tried it in the one next to it. Same result, no red light, no power.

"Hmm..." Emily stood up and tried the switches for the ceiling lights. Both came on as normal.

"Well, that *is* strange," she said in a puzzled voice. "I'm sure the light was on last time I used it."

"Maybe you just didn't notice it," said Simon. "You could have been calling on a dead radio for a while and not realized it."

Emily's heart sank. Could that be it? *Could* she have missed the light being off? Now she wasn't sure; it made her want to cry with the unfairness of it all.

"What do you think is wrong with it?" she asked, looking at him for any sign of hope. "Do you think you can fix it?"

Simon took a deep breath, let it out through his teeth in a whistle, looked at the radio then back at her.

"I tell you what, Emily, if you could rustle up some breakfast, my stomach thinks my throat's been cut. Maybe I could take a look-see under the hood when my guts ain't growling. Whad'ya think, ma'am, is that a plan?"

Emily grinned. "Yes, sir, breakfast, coming right up.

We don't have eggs, but I've got honey to go on the oatmeal and some bread in the freezer."

"And what are you having, do you like oatmeal?"

Emily screwed up her face. "No, I'm bored with oatmeal, even with honey." Her expression brightened. "But we have Pop Tarts!"

"Oh well, you should've said so to start with. Pop Tarts all round then."

After Emily made breakfast for them and a pot of coffee for Simon, she got on with her daily chores while he checked out the radio. She found a few of her dad's tools and showed them to Simon in case they were of any help but he only took one small screwdriver. She put the rest away when she took the bag of clothes to the garbage bin in the store room, where something caught her eye.

She lifted a long strip of grubby material out of the bag. Part of Simon's undershirt, the thick seam from around the neck. Was there something written on it? Like they had to have names on their soccer kit at school. She turned it this way and that in an effort to read it.

R-I-O-B-L? Not any name she recognized, and certainly nothing like Simon. Emily squinted at the writing, trying to make sense of it. Was that an A? then N-C-O

"Rioblanco?" said Emily to herself. "Riob Lanco?" That couldn't be right, could it? And what was the last part?

She rubbed at the dirt with her finger. J, another A, maybe. Jall? Rio Blanco Jail?

"Oh my god!" Emily dropped the piece of cloth as

though it was hot.

"Are you ok?" he was called. He would come looking for her; she had to say something, anything.

"Yes. Yes, don't worry I... I just found we have no more chocolate Pop Tarts. It was a shock, that's all." She held her breath, expecting footsteps any second, but he just laughed.

"Is that all? I think we'll survive. Anyway, I prefer the strawberry ones."

Emily looked at the door to the store room, it was a good solid door and the key was in it. She'd be safe behind that. She crept over as quietly as she could and very, very carefully slid the key out of the lock.

The radio being broken all of a sudden made perfect sense: he must have done something to it so she couldn't call for help.

Emily's heartbeat was twice its normal rate. Her fingers shook as she fitted the key into the inside lock and silently eased the door closed at the same time. It finally swung against the frame, clicked shut and she twisted the key round, stepping back to stare at the door, not knowing what to do next.

Simon

Simon didn't have long now, she'd been too quick to work out something was wrong. He didn't like unfinished business, so she would have to go, that's all there was to it.

He didn't know what had made her cry out just now, but he was damn sure it had nothing to do with Pop

Tarts. So now he held a carving knife from the block in the kitchen, moving as quietly as he could towards the storeroom, alert to the slightest sound that might come from behind the door.

Outside, he pressed his ear up against the wood and stood like that for a minute, listening intently.

Nothing. Silence.

He stood back and reached out with the knife, using the handle to hammer on the door, rattling it in the frame. "Oh, Emily, where are you?" he called, grinning now. "Little pig, little pig, let me in! Hahaha."

No response.

"Come on, you know I'll get in there eventually. Don't make it harder on yourself than it needs to be."

"Go away, I know who you are. Or rather, I know who you aren't." Emily sounded determined, but he heard the fear in her voice. "What happened, did you find a dead body or did you kill someone and take their clothes? I know you've been in jail. It's no use lying anymore, *Simon*, or whatever your name is."

"Aren't you a clever little piggy? Well, it's too late now, missy; I'm going to huff and puff and blow your fucking house down!"

Simon took a step back, then, oblivious to the pain in his foot, kicked the door as hard. The door held fast, the heavy wooden planks more than a match for the impact. Maddened, he took four long strides away from the door, turned and shouted to Emily. "This is your last chance, if you don't come out now, things will be very bad for you indeed."

"I'm warning you," he heard Emily say, "you better go away and not come in here."

"Right, you little bitch," he hissed, his voice rising to a scream as he ran at the door. "COMING, READY OR NOT!"

He slammed into the door, shoulder first. The pain was excruciating. He stared in fury at the door for a second; a bolt of white-hot agony bloomed in his chest and everything went black for the final time.

* ———— ·✠· ———— *

Emily

Emily knew he was up to something. She could almost *hear* him listening out there, but what could he do? Could he get in? She thought he probably would, sooner or later, and she had no illusions about her chances of survival when he did.

She looked frantically around the room, starting to panic now. The gun cabinet! Of course, how could she have been so dumb?

Locked.

A combination padlock hung from a loop in the center of the double door. She sighed with relief. "Thank you, Dad."

She took hold of the lock and then took a deep breath as she forced herself to be calm and spun the numbered reels until they lined up to her date of birth. The lock clicked open. She opened the doors and reached for her father's old bolt action hunting rifle, the one he'd shown her how to use last summer.

A box of ammunition sat in the bottom of the cabinet and she had just loaded a round when Simon yelled outside.

She stood opposite the door and braced the rifle on her shoulder the way Dad had shown her.

"I'm warning you," she said, sounding braver than she felt, "you better go away and not come in here."

The first time he crashed into the door, she was so scared she almost dropped the rifle, certain she was going to die.

The second time, though, Emily was ready. She closed her eyes, and said, "I love you, Dad." And squeezed the trigger.

She stayed in the store room all that day and the following night, just to be sure. Then she unlocked the door and found him where he'd fallen, a single hole in the center of his chest. She knew Dad would have been proud of her for that.

Emily used the plastic groundsheet to drag his body out into the woods behind the cabin, then she tidied up and thought about what to have for dinner.

Or maybe she would wait a little longer before eating. There was a lot to write in her diary today.

New York

Sarah

Kasey Rogers

Dr. Ellison looked over at Sarah in surprise. She'd been about to dismiss the group when Sarah cleared her throat. All eyes were suddenly on the petite woman who'd never spoken in a group session before. Instead of leaving, they all remained seated, waiting to see if Sarah would continue.

She was one of twelve people who sat in a circle in a windowless room off the main corridor in the underground compound. For most of them, this had been home for more than three years. At least, Sarah thought it was three years, and she wasn't sure how long the others had been there; it was hard to recall since there was no reason to mark calendars or account for time anymore. No one was allowed to leave. Even if they wanted to, where would they go?

Sarah scanned the faces of the others and then looked at Dr. Ellison, who nodded her encouragement. Robin and Stacy, too, gave Sarah a knowing look while Alex gave her a slight smile. The others in the group reacted similarly. They had all come to this same moment in their own lives when they finally found the words to tell their story.

Rocking back and forth in her chair—it was time— Sarah looked off toward the door wanting to flee.

Moments passed, but those in the room remained quiet, willing Sarah to persist. She fidgeted with her hands, searching for a place to begin. They all knew what had happened that day in late May. They had lived through it too. But Sarah supposed they had each experienced it differently. And now it was her turn to try to what that day was like for her. Would any of it make sense without knowing about Ethan? she wondered. What about Greg … was their marriage and history together even relevant to what the group expected to hear?

Sarah thought back to that Sunday morning, the one etched in her memory, seated at her favorite restaurant on Manhattan's Lower East Side, enjoying the warmth of the May sunshine. School would be out soon, and she looked forward to spending the summer doing things she'd longed to do for quite some time but never seemed to find the time. Sunday was the first time Sarah had been on her own without her son Ethan in months.

She was dating for the first time since her divorce too. Sam was a teacher she'd met at a conference a while back. She was surprised and quite pleased when he asked her on a date. He taught history at a high school in Queens. She found herself relaxing, knowing she didn't have to worry about getting home or finding a sitter for Ethan. She sipped a Mimosa and studied the menu trying to decide what she wanted.

But telling the group these things wouldn't help them to understand Sarah's anguish. And so she related what happened the night before.

With a hoarse voice, she whispered, "The last words I said to my son Ethan were, 'Are you awake?'" Sarah took a deep breath. "We'd had an argument. Actually, it was more of a fight. He was upset because he was leaving with his father to go to Utah in the morning. He slammed the door to his bedroom, and I heard him ranting alone. When I finally got him to come out for dinner, I explained that I understood his frustration with spending the summer in Utah, but he wasn't having it. He didn't want to go away for the summer. Instead, he wanted to hang out with his friends from school. I think he hated being away from me, too, but he wouldn't tell me that. I told him, "Honey, your dad and I agreed. I get you all year, but daddy has you at Christmas and all summer. And the only reason you're going a week earlier is that your father is coming East for a friend's wedding, and he wanted to fly with you to Utah instead of having me put you on a plane by yourself. Aren't you excited about seeing Nana and Poppy? What about going to Yellowstone? I've never even been! Daddy will take you with him on his seniors' class trip! Isn't that cool? You'll get to hang out with all these big kids and ride on the bus with them. Doesn't that sound like fun?"

"Instead of being happy about spending time with Greg, Ethan refused to speak to me for the rest of the night and even the following morning. He gave me the cold shoulder. When I woke him up, Ethan wouldn't eat breakfast and just grabbed his suitcase and handed it to Greg when he arrived. I tried to kiss Ethan goodbye, but he rushed out the door. Part of me wanted to call after him to say I was sorry. But I didn't because I was tired of apologizing for things I didn't do wrong. He'd been such a little shit all week, and I had every right to call him out for it. I was too angry to say anything by that point. I watched them disappear into the elevator, and neither one looked back. Even when Greg called me to tell me they'd arrived in Salt Lake, Ethan refused to get on the phone."

Images of Ethan flooded Sarah's memory. Although he was twelve at the time, Sarah pictured him as an infant. Then his sweet toothless smile came to mind, the one she captured and framed when he was six and dressed as Spider-Man for Halloween. She'd always thought they were close, but Ethan changed when she and Greg divorced. Suddenly he wouldn't do his homework, and even getting him to take a shower or stay off his computer led to endless fighting. He started calling her a bitch under his breath.

Then it occurred to Sarah that maybe Ethan wasn't the only one who changed. She had changed too. Sarah barely remembered who she was before she got married. She was always stressed trying to be that perfect wife and mother. But unfortunately, none of her efforts seemed to pay off, and Greg found ways to make her doubt so much of herself, her abilities.

"I was at a restaurant on the Lower East Side having brunch when the eruption happened," she said, looking at those in the group. "Minutes before the sirens went off, I heard my cellphone ring, and I assumed it my ex-husband calling." Sarah didn't bother explaining that she had the ringtone for Greg's number set to Chopin's 'Funeral March.' She always knew when it was him.

She remembered thinking he was probably calling to chew her out for something. She had tried to think back to the night before. Did she pack enough underwear for Ethan? Did his have his extra inhaler? Was Ethan behaving? Then she was angry because all she wanted was to have one morning to enjoy herself.

But then it occurred to her that maybe it was Ethan calling and he was using Greg's phone. "I didn't want to answer it because I knew if I spoke to Ethan, I'd let him off the hook even though he'd been acting like such a brat. I debated for a minute but then gave in and decided to answer it. But by that time, my cell phone had stopped ringing. A moment later, I saw there was a voicemail. I looked at Sam to comment on it, and that's when the sirens went off.

"Everyone on the patio was looking at one another. Someone shouted something about a terrorist attack, and we all panicked. I was very young when 9/11 happened. Maybe because my family lived in Manhattan, I'd always expected it would happen again. It's hard not to recall the chaos that surrounded us at that moment. It was complete pandemonium. Not because Manhattan was the epicenter of it all this time.

But because even those who were born after 9/11 happened grew up knowing New York was a possible strike target and that it could happen at any time.

"The restaurant was just a few blocks from where the Twin Towers once stood. I couldn't move. Sam grabbed my hand, yanked me from my chair, and headed toward Spring Street and the subway. I'd left my phone on the table and turned back to get it. Sam was furious with me.

"Sarah, don't be ridiculous!" he told me.

"But what if Ethan calls again?" I ignored him and turned back. A lady sitting at the table next to us at the restaurant ran up and handed me my phone. We ran back toward the subway station at Spring Street. Sam was gone. By the time we got to the Spring Street entrance, there was a sea of people all going underground. No one knew what was happening, but we were all heading in the same direction. Hours later, we learned that the Super Volcano at Yellowstone had erupted."

Every person in the room knew what had happened immediately after the eruption. Much of life was wiped out for hundreds of miles surrounding Yellowstone. But in the following months, the impact still ravaged the rest of the country. Ash damaged millions of buildings. Sewage and water lines were blocked. Livestock and crops died. Planes couldn't fly, and people couldn't drive. The cascading impact of the eruption left many places within the States uninhabitable. Those who managed to survive only did so by finding refuge in places that already existed underground. In the aftermath, many spaces were converted to make-shift housing, but strictly controlled to prevent a further loss of human life.

Sarah looked around. The solemn look on the faces of those surrounding her spoke of their understanding of her misery. She had heard each of their stories. They'd witnessed horrors she could barely comprehend and did everything within their power to survive. And yet, they listened intently, waiting for her to continue.

"We were in that subway for a long time. I don't even know how many days. Though we were safe, we were also trapped. Those who were underground were afraid to leave because we knew that the air was toxic because of the ash. It was hard to breathe, and nothing was operating anyway. There was no one to rescue us. Sometimes those who left came back and told of the devastation. Rumors were flying. We heard that many people had fled the City by then. The only comfort I had was getting to know Ruth. She was the woman who gave me back my cellphone. The two of us stuck together as long as we could."

Sarah's voice trailed off as she recalled the worst parts of her ordeal. The intense hunger and thirst were hard to bear, as were the endless days in darkness and sleepless nights. That wasn't the worst of it. "I kept wondering what had happened to Ethan."

The unplayed message on her phone might yield a clue, but the battery had died long before she had a chance to listen to it. Cell phones had become obsolete before she could recharge it. So she had no way to retrieve the message. That made it easier to believe they had somehow survived, and she might find them someday.

That kind of thinking was unrealistic, but it kept her from dwelling on trying to imagine what had really happened to her son and his father. Those in the group described their experiences in vivid detail, and Sarah was glad she didn't have flashbacks and nightmares like many others. They were so hard to listen to.

One of the survivors, a woman named Melody, who was part of another group, was consumed by thoughts of not doing enough to save her little girl. The staff watched her carefully but one day, she was gone. Everyone was told she had found a way to escape. While Dr. Ellison repeated this explanation, Robin, or maybe it was Stacey, revealed she'd been found in a pool of blood one morning. She had escaped. But not the way Dr. Ellison implied.

From then on, Sarah did everything in her power to forget as much as possible. Yet she was constantly lost in thoughts about Ethan. It never went away; it was something she had to confront before it consumed her.

Sarah was quiet for a moment before she shifted in her chair. Then, finally, she planted her feet on the floor. The words suddenly couldn't come fast enough: they had to be expelled as quickly as possible. "He shouldn't have been there," she cried.

"What do you mean?" Dr. Ellison asked her.

"When Greg told me he was coming East for the wedding, I begged him to take Ethan back to Utah early. He refused at first because of his class trip to Yellowstone. "Ethan would love that," I told him. "He's really excited about seeing your parents this summer. He even mentioned he wished he could go early." Greg ate it up. I'd learned that arguing with Greg got me nowhere—so I lied. He wanted to believe me, and before I knew it, he'd rearranged his flight so he could pick up Ethan and acted as though it was all his idea."

Tears ran down Sarah's face. "I was so tired of fighting with him. I wanted my son to go. I wanted Ethan to get on that plane with Greg. Don't you see? When Ethan left with his father, a part of me was glad to see him go. Now I'll never know what would have happened if I'd just told Greg the truth."

A silence fell over the room. Then, finally, Dr. Ellison spoke. "It's easy to second guess ourselves, isn't it, group?" The others nodded but remained silent. "You've taken a big step, Sarah, and we're all very proud of you. I think we've accomplished a great deal tonight. As everyone rose to leave, Dr. Ellison reminded them, "We'll meet again tomorrow, at the same time. And Sarah, the next time, maybe you can be the one to start?"

Downingtown, PA

Laurel

By Laura Berry

We had a clear day today! Well – clearish. The ash in the air dulls everything to a point where you'd swear it's winter even though we're barely into fall, but hey, the sun coming through was enough to warm my cheeks. Right now, that's good enough.

It sounds weird to say, but I'm actually grateful Covid came when it did. Noble and I gathered quite the face-mask stash during the height of the toilet-paper-rustling era of the pandemic. So today, as the sun shone tepidly through the ash clouds, we stuck on two face masks each and went out to soak in some rays. I don't know if double-masking is genuinely doing anything to protect us, but I swear we'd start hallucinating if we hadn't broken out of what we now call the clunker bunker for some "fresh" air.

The constant ash-swirling threat of terrible air quality has been hard on the dogs, so they were happy for the chance to go out and play. We didn't bother with their leashes much since no one else was outside. Coop got to chase a ball for the first time in what honestly may have been weeks. Poor guy. Old stinky Sally was happy enough to paw through the mix of ash and fallen leaves. Like I said. She's old. She's just happy she wakes up from her naps these days.

The four of us didn't wander too far from the house. It isn't safe to stay outside too long obviously, but it was such a relief to be out of the house. Noble's job keeps him busy on the phone (when there's reception), and when the internet connection is good, I can get some writing done. It does feel like we spend most of our time languishing in our living room though, watching for a blue sky, like kids watching for Santa. That's why I still consider this a good day, even though Coop decided to pee on Sally's head as she was sniffing at something on the ground.

Oh! Yesterday we had a treat too. We were able to get the car started – turning our extra sheets into a car cover was maybe one of the smartest things we did right after the eruption – and we made it to the hospital to see my sister. I could only wave at her through the window. I understand why cancer patients have to be kept in isolation now, but it's still, just, sad. I think she appreciated seeing us. It's hard to tell with the oxygen mask if she was smiling or not. She did lift her hand to wave. That's something I guess.

Now for some of the more troublesome news … I

should have asked Noble to take me to the store on the way home from the hospital. There's hardly any good candy left which is really a disappointment, because if I have to live through the apocalypse, I should at least have access to some decent bonbons. Yes, I said bonbons. Let me be fancy. I miss being fancy sometimes.

Anyway. Yesterday. I've been feeling off and of course I had my IUD taken out three months ago. In my defense, it was about to expire before the eruption, but now, here we are with ash coating everything, gas prices going crazy (because price gouging is still happening), and intermittent access to the internet. Doesn't really make getting to the gyno's for a new IUD easy. And, well, currently my stomach feels – off. If what's happening is what I think is happening, I'm going to stop being human and simply erupt into a ball of fury and, honestly, mourning. A post-pandemic, possibly pre-second civil war America I could handle with a baby. I mean, I wanted to have one. But this? This constant gray sky, essentially no access to a doctor, AND a pre-second-civil-war America? Come on. I should be able to give a kid a chance at least.

So. Here's hoping I'm not pregnant even though that's what I've freaking wanted for the last year. Here's hoping I don't have to take care of the problem. I was going to name our baby Landel. It's a combination of our names, Laurel and Noble. Noble's cutting wit and my charm would make one hell of a person. Can you imagine? Our kid would grow up to be an absolute heartbreaker. And if Landel were anything like me, probably an absolutely delightful idiot, too.

I would have liked to meet Landel. But, hey – the sky was a little clear today. Small miracles, right?

That's all, I suppose for this journal entry. I'll have to see what tomorrow brings.

Dick and Joan Jacobs Public Interest Environmental Law Clinic

Dick and his wife, Joan, have made a generous gift and a significant portion of their estate to establish the Dick and Joan Jacobs Public Interest Environmental Law Clinic and the Institute for Environmental Justice at Stetson University College of Law. The Institute will provide governmental organizations, as well as legal and non-legal communities, with a wide variety of environmental law-related public interest services — while molding law students to become the difference makers to care for Mother Earth. Additional funds are needed to secure the Institute in order for it to produce the long-term, positive results the Jacobs's envision.

If you would like to make an additional donation to this charity, you can at:
https://www.stetson.edu/law/forms/jacobs.php